THE
FUNICULAR

A MARTIN TAYLOR ART CRIME ADVENTURE

John R. Aarons

The Funicular
A Martin Taylor Art Crime Adventure

Copyright © 2023 by John R. Aarons

Paperback ISBN: 978-1-63812-604-1
Hardcover ISBN: 978-1-63812-609-6
Ebook ISBN: 978-1-63812-605-8

All rights reserved. No part in this book may be produced and transmitted in any form or by any means, electronic, or mechanical, including photocopying, recording, or by any information storage and retrieval system, without permission in writing from the copyright owner.

The views expressed in this work are solely those of the author and do not necessarily reflect the views of the publisher hereby disclaims any responsibility for them.

Published by Pen Culture Solutions   02/08/2023

Pen Culture Solutions
1-888-727-7204 (USA)
1-800-950-458 (Australia)
support@penculturesolutions.com

Other books by this Author:

The Docklands Mystery
The Maltese Cross Mystery
The Houston Art Chronicles

Fulfillment of my great Australian Dream
Memoirs of a Lifetime of Travelling the World

CHAPTER 1

OCTOBER 11, BILBA O, SPAIN

After purchasing a token from the man in the ticket booth, Martin boarded the sharply angled railcar and sat facing downward in a compartment at the lower end of the carriage to have the best view of Bilbao as it climbed slowly towards the summit of Mount Artxanda, approximately 400 metres above the sprawling city. The grade of the track is especially steep, so the funicular moves at a reasonably comfortable pace. There is only a single track, and about halfway up there is a passing bay to allow a second train coming down to loop around the one going in the opposite direction. The two drivers are in two-way radio contact to co-ordinate the departure times at both ends.

Martin was fascinated by the experience as he had never seen a funicular railway or even heard of them before. There is certainly nothing like it in the city he calls home. He had bought a top quality camera at the airport duty free shop before departing Melbourne and was now turning from side to side snapping photos of the wonderful views as the train crawled upwards at what seemed to be no more than a brisk walking pace.

At the passing bay, he turned to watch an almost empty train slide slowly by and just before it disappeared altogether, he saw two figures struggling in the uppermost compartment. Straining to get a better look, he suddenly heard what he believed was the muffled sound of a gunshot.

As a senior detective with the Victorian Police Force back home in Melbourne, Australia, Martin had undergone considerable firearms training at the Police Academy in Glen Waverley. He was certain that what he had just heard was definitely a shot fired from a gun with a noise suppressor attached.

There was nothing he could do to alert anyone, as passengers and the driver of the train were in separate closed off compartments so he had to wait till they reached the summit.

Once the train stopped, he ran up to the driver but immediately discovered that he didn't understand a word of English. Martin took out his mobile phone and with gestures reminiscent of a game of charades, asked the driver to call the police.

The Spanish word for police is close enough for the driver to understand his request and he immediately dialled 112 which is the emergency services telephone number, and passed the phone back to Martin.

When someone answered and asked in Spanish if he wanted police, ambulance or fire brigade. Martin recognized the word *'policia'* and asked to be connected to that department. Within seconds he found himself speaking with the receptionist at the Bilbao Municipal Police Force who fortunately was conversant enough in English to understand what he was saying. He explained that he urgently needed to speak to someone in the homicide division who was able to speak English. He was put through immediately to a man speaking excellent English.

"Good morning sir, I am the Chief Inspector of the Bilbao Police Department.

I wouldn't normally take incoming calls related to daily police matters, but the telephone operator said that you had asked in English for the homicide division and she said that from the tone of your voice it must be a serious matter. That is why I decided to personally take your call. Please tell me in detail of your concerns so I can decide on the best way to assist you."

Martin explained, "My name is Martin Taylor and I am a visiting Australian police officer holidaying in Bilbao. I believe that I may have witnessed a shooting a few minutes ago on the funicular. The train on which the incident occurred is now at the lower street level but I am at the top station standing with the driver of the train I was on. Unfortunately he doesn't understand English so I have been unable to explain to him what I saw occur on the descending train."

The Chief Inspector then replied, "Please pass your phone to the train driver so I can give him instructions as to what he is to do until we arrive. He will be asked to lead you out of the station at the top and you are to wait there for one of my men to come by and pick you up." Martin handed his phone to the driver who listened intently for a few moments then passed the phone back to him. Using his two-way radio, he immediately called his counterpart on the other train at street level. "Hey Juan, this is Fidel, I have just been speaking with the Chief of Police and apparently there's been some sort of incident on your train. An English speaking tourist had asked me to call the police and after they had talked for a few minutes, I was ordered to have the gates locked to prevent anyone trying to leave or enter the station and told to pass on these instructions to you immediately."

The driver took a deep breath and continued, "The only exception was to be the tourist who was instructed to wait outside the funicular station at the top until a police car came to collect him."

The driver led Martin to the street outside the station and with a few Spanish words and gestures, told him to wait for the police there. He then returned inside the station and locked the gate. The only word Martin understood was *'policia'* and anyway, the Chief Inspector had told him to wait there to be picked up.

Within minutes, the funicular had been shut down and the entrances top and bottom closed off by large wrought iron gates. Unfortunately, the few passengers that had been on the descending train had departed long before the order was given to close the gates.

While Martin waited, his mind went back to earlier that morning when he had set off from the hotel looking for the funicular and how it was that he was now in Bilbao, a city he knew nothing about until recently. Meanwhile, he soaked up the spectacular views over the city and took some more photos to add to the growing collection of pictures he had from his recent visit to Madrid.

Martin's plan for the day was to ride the funicular to the lookout at the top of the mountain because he had been told the view was spectacular and then go back down and visit the Guggenheim Museum.

This architectural wonder appeared even more spectacular from the lookout than from the ground as he could now see the complete structure in relation to the surroundings. There was a colourful bridge running alongside the museum so close it appeared to be an integral part of the overall design. There was a considerable amount of traffic flowing over the bridge so it was obviously a major arterial road enabling people to get to and from this part of town.

The funicular railway is located in the old quarter of Bilbao a couple of blocks in from the river with an unobtrusive entrance tucked away between some nondescript buildings. There are a couple of cafes and bars nearby but there appeared to be little else of interest. It's not an easy place to find for tourists because there are no obvious signs leading to it and it seemed to Martin that the locals wanted to keep this little gem all to themselves. In any case, it had been constructed to provide a quick and inexpensive way for people living at the top of the mountain to get to their places of employment or to the department stores in the city.

Fortunately, Martin had been given clear directions on how to find it by the concierge at the Gran Hotel Domine where he was staying, directly opposite the Guggenheim Museum. He had taken the smart looking tram that ran past the hotel into the centre of the old town, and then walked along narrow streets following the route on the map that the concierge had marked out for him. The town was filled with graceful old buildings, some with planter boxes hanging from the upper storey windows that were overflowing with multi-coloured flowers to brighten up the otherwise dull facades.

As he wandered the streets he paused every now and then to look in shop windows, marvelling at the old world memorabilia on display.

Whenever he ventured inside one of them, he found the people friendly and helpful to this visitor from the other side of the world.

He stopped for a coffee and a snack in a small café-bar called El Picasso. He chatted with the barman who spoke excellent English. The early morning rush to grab a coffee and snack on the way to the office was over so there weren't many customers in the café at that time. Being the relatively quiet time before the next busy rush for lunch, the barman was happy to talk to Martin. He introduced himself as Pablo proudly announcing that he had been named after Picasso, the famous Spanish artist. Martin asked him how he had learned to speak English so well and Pablo replied that after he finished school, he had travelled to England and worked in a couple of pubs for 6 months before returning home. He was keen to talk to Martin about the history of this region and explained, "Because the local Basque people were staunchly republican, they were badly treated by the Nationalists who had taken over the running of Spain during the 1930's under the leadership of the ruthless dictator, General Francisco Franco. Together with assistance from Hitler and Mussolini, General Franco started a civil war in 1936 against the Republicans who were backed by Stalin's Soviet Union and leftist volunteers from places as far flung as South America."

He went on to say, "The famous American author Ernest Hemingway, who absolutely adored the Spanish way of life before the civil war, was among the foreign Republican supporters. He was a regular visitor to Spain and never missed a bullfight when he was here. The civil war in Spain gave Hitler an opportunity to provide first hand training for his troops. In particular, it proved crucial for the expanding German air force he had put together for the much larger campaign he was planning elsewhere in Europe. His pilots gained plenty of bombing practice on Spanish cities during this terrible war which dragged on for three long years."

After pouring another cup of coffee for Martin he went on, "One of the worst hit regions was the Basque country because of its backing of the royal family and a democratic, albeit somewhat leftist form of government. The nearby city of Guernica was completely wiped out by German warplanes in a saturated bombing raid that killed thousands. Many of my family including my grandparents were killed at that time."

The barman became more animated as he pointed to a photograph of the famous Picasso painting *'Guernica'* that was hanging on the wall behind the bar. "It's a mammoth work some three and a half metres long which depicts the slaughter of the residents and the complete destruction of the city of Guernica by the German bombers. Unfortunately, the original painting is currently hanging in the Queen Sofia Museum in Madrid so we Basques don't get to see it unless we make the long and expensive journey to Madrid."

Martin managed to squeeze in a few words at this point, "I saw that magnificent painting when I was in Madrid last weekend. As it happens, I am very involved in the world of art, not as a collector but as an Australian policeman tracking down stolen paintings and the criminals responsible for the theft or fraudulent sale of stolen artworks."

Pablo paused to pour himself a small glass of Tequila and continued in an emotional voice...... "The Guernica painting should be on display here in the old Bilbao Art and History Museum. My fellow countrymen from the Basque region have for years been petitioning the government in Madrid to have it brought here but unfortunately, our pleas have fallen on deaf ears. It is such a famous and valuable piece of art, our illustrious leaders want it to stay in Madrid where it can bring in large amounts of money from the millions of tourists that visit our capital every year."

Martin paid for his snack and thanked him for the history lesson and headed off again looking for the funicular station. It turned out to be only a couple of blocks further on at the Plaza Funicular. At that moment he had no idea that he was about to take a ride that would change his ideas of having a peaceful holiday forever!

....

It was less than a 10 minute wait following Martin's telephone call with the Bilbao Chief Inspector before a dark green Renault police car with flashing red and blue lights screeched to a stop outside the funicular station. He was the only person standing by the locked gate when the uniformed officer jumped out, saluted a greeting and opened the rear door for Martin to climb in. He was driven at high speed down the winding road to the bottom of the mountain and the car stopped outside the funicular entrance which was now roped off with crime-scene tape.

As Martin got out from the car, a tall handsome man with a pencil thin moustache and wearing a sharp dark grey suit approached with hand outstretched. He introduced himself as Inspector Joseba Segueras, Chief of Police for the city of Bilbao. Martin was escorted into the funicular ticket office which had been cleared for the police to use as their temporary investigation headquarters.

They sat down at a bare table in the staff lunch room and Chief Inspector Segueras asked some questions whilst one of his assistants took notes.

Martin firstly gave them his full name and address in Australia as well as the name of the hotel where he was staying in Bilbao. He then explained that he was a Detective Senior Sergeant with the Fraud Squad at the Victorian Police Headquarters in Melbourne, Australia.

"I've been in Madrid this past week attending an international conference on art fraud which I found to be extremely interesting and enlightening.

I then spent the weekend in Madrid visiting the magnificent Prado, the Reina Sofia Museum and went twice to the museum housing the Thyssen-Bornemisza Collection." He continued, "As I had some vacation time owing, I decided to extend my stay in Spain and visit the Guggenheim Museum before facing the long flight back to Australia."

Finding his throat quite dry, Martin asked for a glass of water before continuing...... "I only arrived in Bilbao yesterday and haven't yet visited the Museum. Luckily I have been able to gaze at this architectural masterpiece from my hotel room on the third floor as it looks directly out at the gleaming titanium structure. I really want to explore the museum's collections and look at any special exhibition they might have on display at the moment."

Chief Inspector Segueras elaborated on their findings so far, "When we arrived at the funicular station after your call, the train you had witnessed the struggle in remained parked at the bottom as per our instructions. The driver told us that he has been preparing to go back up again totally unaware that anything had happened on his train a short time before. He was shocked when he was told by the other driver at the top that he had helped an English speaking passenger contact the police on his mobile phone and was ordered to close the main gates immediately. He assumed that the tourist might have had his wallet lifted by a gypsy, something which unfortunately is not unusual in Spain."

The Chief Inspector continued, "The driver was extremely surprised to see a squad of police arrive and take over the entire funicular operation. He couldn't imagine that this level of police involvement was just because some tourist had been robbed. He became very nervous and upset when I told him that there may have been a shooting on his train as it was descending the mountain. As you had observed, the carriages are made up of separate compartments with the driver located in his own little cubicle at the bottom. He wouldn't have seen or heard anything happening in a compartment at the top of the train. It wasn't long before our search of the train revealed a body slumped on the floor in the top compartment. Not surprisingly, there wasn't any sign of the perpetrator or a weapon. The murdered man had died of a single gunshot wound to the head and when searched, the police were unable to find any identification. His pockets were completely empty."

Martin was asked if he could describe the assailant. "I only saw the two men struggling for a couple of seconds as the trains passed. My view was partly blocked by the angled wall of the carriage which matches the slope of the incline. Despite this, my police training has resulted in my being able to spontaneously take note of certain characteristics and I am able to confirm the following….. the attacker was a Caucasian male, of fair complexion with a full head of long blonde hair tied in a ponytail. I estimate the height of the man to be close to 2 metres, which would make him stand out in a crowd. I also noticed some dark markings on the backs of the man's hands which I suggest might be tattoos."

Chief Inspector Segueras then asked Martin, "If necessary, would you be able to extend your stay in Spain for a short while to help in the investigation as you are the sole witness to the murder? You could be very useful in assisting us with our inquiries. You might find it interesting to work with us and compare how we handle criminal investigations of this nature with your methods in Australia."

Martin considered the proposal for a moment and replied, "I still have 5 days of vacation left and would be happy to use some of that time to assist in any way I can. If it turns out that you want me to stay longer than my allocated vacation time, we would have to request permission from my superiors back in Melbourne. I came to Bilbao specifically to visit the

Guggenheim Museum and despite all that has happened today I am still looking forward to going there in the next day or so."

"I think that should be plenty of time for us to wrap up this case," said the Chief Inspector somewhat optimistically, little knowing what lay ahead of them!

Martin was driven back to his hotel in a police car and was told that he would be picked up at 8.30 the following morning to be taken to the Municipal Police Headquarters which is located in the centre of the city. They would like him to look through some photos of known criminals operating in this area.

He spent a quiet evening in the hotel, dining alone in the restaurant then went to his room and emailed friends and colleagues back home to tell them of the recent events. The bathroom in his suite had a glass wall that enabled him to see the Guggenheim Museum through the bedroom window whilst luxuriating in a warm bath. The museum was subtly illuminated at night giving the titanium cladding an almost ghostly appearance. He ran over in his mind everything he'd seen during the day and tried to recall anything that might help in the investigation.

Before climbing into bed somewhat exhausted from everything that had happened during this very unusual day, he began to recall the events of the previous month when the reason for his visit to Spain began

....

CHAPTER 2

SEPTEMBER 1, MELBOURNE, AUSTRALIA

At the Victorian Police Complex conveniently located on St.Kilda Road, an elegant tree-lined boulevard just outside the Melbourne CBD, a top level gathering was in progress in a large meeting room on an upper floor of this modern high rise office building. The meeting was being run by the Chief Commissioner, Sir Charles MacPherson, and was attended by senior members of the art crime division of the fraud squad. He had received his knighthood some years earlier when he was the head of Scotland Yard in London. He had subsequently been offered the position he now held as Chief Commissioner of the Victorian Police. He thanked the team for their efforts over the past year, highlighting that the department had solved all but one out of more than 12 major art crimes during this period. "Your diligence brought to trial two highly organised crime syndicates. They had been involved in multi-million dollar scams that had defrauded some of the country's top business people."

The Chief Commissioner went on to say, "The officer in charge during these operations was Detective Sergeant Martin

Taylor and as a result of his excellent work, it is my pleasure to announce today that he has been promoted to Detective Senior Sergeant."

The people around the table all turned to Martin and congratulated him before the Chief Commissioner asked for some quiet as he had another announcement to make.

"We have recently received an invitation to send a delegate to an international symposium on art fraud and theft that is being held in Madrid during October.

This symposium is expected to be of significant importance as it is to be run by a group of senior people from Interpol and the FBI Art Loss Register.

The State Government has requested that one of our top police officers be selected to attend and after some deliberation, the State Minister of Police and myself have selected Martin to be the person to go to Madrid and take part in the conference." He finished up by saying, "So Martin, make sure your passport is current because arrangements are under way for you to fly to Madrid at the end of the month!"

A humble Martin stood up and responded, "I wish to thank the Chief Commissioner for my promotion and promise to do my best to show the delegates at the symposium that we in Australia are up there with the world's best policing methods."

The symposium was to run for a week between the first and seventh of October and a representative of each delegation had been requested to present a paper on their most recent experiences with art crime in their country.

This was a huge step up the ladder for the 36 year old Martin who had been in the police force for 15 years after graduating from the Victorian Police Academy. His travels outside Australia previously had been limited to a two week vacation in a popular holiday resort on the Indonesian island of Bali and a couple of days in Auckland, New Zealand following up a lead on a stolen painting the year before.

This would be his first trip to Europe so he was especially thrilled to have been chosen to attend the symposium in Madrid.

Martin's passport was valid for another 5 years and as Australians do not require visas to visit Spain that made his travel plans easy.

He spent a large part of his time over the ensuing weeks preparing his presentation and gathering data concerning relevant cases that he could include in his speech. During his spare time, he borrowed a copy from his local library of the *'Lonely Planet'* travel book on Madrid and started reading it to plan what he could do with the time he would have outside of the conference. He decided to take a week from his annual vacation time and check out some of the sights before returning home.

He would now be able to sample some of the paintings on display at the museums in Madrid that would be his first foray into European art on its home territory.

It was important for his work that he kept abreast of what was happening in the art world and his department subscribed to a number of art magazines published in Australia as well as

Europe and the USA. He remembered reading an article in the Melbourne *'Age'* newspaper that commented on Spain and Portugal feeling neglected during the post Second World War boom years when new art galleries and museums were being built in other countries throughout the 1980's. Suddenly money was made available from private institutions and savings banks, and top architects were employed to design and build a spate of new museums around Spain. One of the grandest of these was the Reina Sofia in Madrid which opened in 1990. He made a note in his diary to make sure he found time to visit this museum.

Following the World Financial Crisis just a few years ago, money dried up for these museums to purchase new items to expand their collections. Local artists began moving to other countries seeking to promote their work.

Fortunately, the major European museums and galleries have retained excellent collections. Some of Martin's colleagues who had travelled extensively, told him that there are long queues of visitors every day at all of these great institutions.

Since he had moved to the fraud squad and was attached to the art crime division, he had studied and accumulated a considerable knowledge of art, particularly paintings and sculpture. During his weekends off, he had visited most of the State Galleries and Museums in Australia and many of the excellent regional galleries in the larger Victorian country cities. All have considerable collections of Australian art and others such as the National Gallery of Australia in Canberra and the National Gallery of Victoria, known as the NGV, have reasonable, albeit relatively small collections of European paintings by famous artists. There was the brazen theft from the NGV in Melbourne in August 1986 of a Picasso painting called *'Weeping Woman'*. It was an early version of a number of portraits of Dora Maar, a well know photographer of the 1930's and one of Picasso's muses. The Gallery had purchased the painting in 1985 for 1.6 million dollars which was at that time a record amount for an Australian public art gallery to pay for a painting.

Everyone connected to the gallery as well as police were baffled how something like this theft could have taken place. Despite very tight security, it had just mysteriously vanished off the wall! It turned up some time later in a locker at a Melbourne railway station undamaged and was promptly returned to its rightful place in the Gallery. The perpetrators were never found but a note left with the painting written by a group calling itself the *'Australian Cultural Terrorists'* requested the government to increase its annual funding for the arts!

In the future, Martin intended to visit all of the great museums in the world such as the Louvre in Paris, the Metropolitan Museum in New York, the Tate in London, the Rijksmuseum in Amsterdam and the Hermitage in St.Petersberg, the latter having one of the most comprehensive and largest art collections in the world.

For now though, he was excited about his upcoming trip to Spain and the opportunity to visit the Prado Museum in Madrid of which he had heard and read so much about.

Martin's father, Harry had also been a policeman and was a senior figure in the Homicide Squad in Melbourne during the 1950's and 60's when the local branch of the Italian Mafia controlled the lucrative Footscray wholesale fruit and vegetable market. Gang wars were common throughout that period and it was not unusual for men to be shot as they walked out their front door in the morning, waving goodbye to their wives as they headed off to the sell their fruit and vegs at the market.

For many years the State Government has been trying to rid this organization of the Mafia influence and eventually built an entirely new wholesale market in an outer suburb. They closed the old market down and believe they can now better control the entire operation and keep a close watch on how the place is managed.

Unfortunately, Sergeant Harry Taylor died some years ago whilst attempting to arrest a Mafia gang boss named Alphonso Cardamone, long suspected of being the head of a huge drug smuggling operation. He was mortally wounded after being shot in the chest by the criminal's bodyguard. The killer was never apprehended and it was suspected that he and Cardamone were on an aeroplane headed back to Sicily within hours of the shooting. As is usually the case in these situations, there were no witnesses willing to speak to the detectives when they arrived at the market to investigate the shooting.

Martin's mother was proud of her husband's police record and was pleased when Martin joined the Victorian force. On the day he graduated from the Police Academy, she hugged him and whispered in his ear, "Please don't volunteer to work in the homicide division Martin, it's far too dangerous. I don't want to lose a second member of my family!"

Martin's sister, Barbara is a successful lawyer and is a partner in a large Melbourne law firm specializing in white collar crime cases. She has occasionally called on Martin for advice in fraud cases where the distinction between what is lawful and what is not can sometimes be considered a grey area. Although they don't always see eye to eye in these situations, they are nonetheless very close and have a very happy and friendly relationship. She was one of the first to congratulate him on his promotion today.

He wondered what his mother would think of the situation her son from the Victorian Fraud Squad now found himself in. Firstly as a delegate at a world symposium on art crime in Madrid, then holidaying in Northern Spain and suddenly finding himself part of a murder investigation in a Spanish city so far from home! On the one hand she would undoubtedly feel proud of his involvement but on the other hand, as he was the only witness to a murder, she would be extremely concerned for his safety.

CHAPTER 3

SEPTEMBER 29, MELBOURNE, AUSTRALIA – MADRID, SPAIN, SEPTEMBER 30.

Martin Taylor departed Melbourne Airport mid-afternoon on a Thai Airlines 10 hour flight to Bangkok where he had to change planes for a direct flight to Madrid. Sitting in the departure lounge at Bangkok's Suvarnabhumi international terminal waiting for the onward flight to Spain, he picked up an in-flight magazine to read. Most of the articles were about travel in places not on his itinerary but one article caught his attention. The journalist wrote in glowing terms about a city called Bilbao in the Basque region of northern Spain. The city and its surroundings had until not long ago, been a run-down industrial area with a mostly disused port and crumbling old buildings lining the river bank.

In the 1990's, the Guggenheim Foundation in New York, had selected Bilbao as the city to build a new museum and had chosen the renowned Canadian architect, Frank Gehry to design something special that would really give this old city a boost. According to the magazine article, the result was truly spectacular and in 1997 the museum opened to world-wide acclaim, winning a number of prestigious architectural awards. The city of Bilbao underwent a reformation and has since become one of the '*must visit*' places in Europe for travellers from all around the world.

The original Guggenheim Museum was designed by the famous American architect Frank Lloyd Wright and was built on 5th Avenue in New York. It opened in 1959 and unfortunately Frank Lloyd Wright had passed away shortly before construction had been completed. The museum was unlike any others and became a landmark for visitors to New York. Obviously, the museum in Bilbao has followed in the same footsteps as the original being of unique design.

He was so taken by the magazine article, that by the time he was called to board his onward flight, Martin had made up his mind to travel to Bilbao after the forum ended. He wanted to see for himself what this city of Bilbao was all about and, because of his special interest in art, he was particularly keen to see the Guggenheim Museum. Little did he know then how that spur of the moment decision would turn out to have such an impact on his life!

His flight took off just after midnight and travelled through the night arriving at Madrid International Airport around 8.00am which meant because he had to turn his watch back to the local time, he had been flying for another 12 hours. By the time he had cleared Customs and Immigration, it was mid-morning and after he collected his suitcase form the carousel, he noticed a chauffeur holding up a sign with his name on. The police travel agent who had booked his flights had also arranged for a driver to take him to his hotel on arrival in Madrid. After a pleasant drive through suburbs mostly built up with high-rise apartment blocks, he arrived at the Hotel Reina de Madrid in the centre of the city, not far from the Conference Centre where the forum was to be held.

Although he would have liked nothing better than to have gone to his room to sleep off some of the jetlag he was experiencing, the clerk at the desk informed him that the room was not yet ready. He was told that it would be available after 2.00pm. He checked his baggage with the hotel porter and went for a walk.

Without actually knowing anything yet about the hotel's location he found that just around the corner from the hotel was an impressive wide tree-lined avenue called Paseo Del Prado. This turned out to be the main thoroughfare of Madrid. He took a note of the building on the corner so he could recognise the side street when he returned to the hotel later. Wandering along the avenue in glorious autumn sunshine, he soon found himself enjoying the hustle and bustle of this vibrant city.

One of his friends back in Australia who regularly travelled abroad for vacations, had given him advice on the best way to get over jetlag. "From my years of flying around the world, as soon as you arrive at your destination in another country, walk around for a couple of hours and let the body acclimatise to the new time zone." This was what Martin was now doing and so far he was feeling good.

He stopped outside a bank and withdrew some Euros from the ATM then sat down at an outdoor café relishing in the warm sunlight and fresh air after all those hours cooped up on the aeroplane. Being a tourist strip, the waiter spoke English and recommended a Spanish omelette with salad and a glass of local wine. Watching the constant stream of people passing by, he was struck by how well dressed in the smartest fashions they were, and decided he would lash out and buy a new outfit for himself to smarten up his own appearance.

Following an enjoyable brunch, he continued walking along the avenue and came across a fascinating area beneath an overpass where some modern sculptures had been installed to brighten up what otherwise would have been dead space under the roadway. There was even an attractive water feature. He spent some time there admiring the sculptures and thinking what a great way to make use of what otherwise would just be an area to collect fallen leaves and the detritus that is generally found piling up in a large city like this. He then continued his walk along the avenue taking in the beauty of the marvellous old buildings that lined both sides of the road. After a couple of hours, he thought to himself, *'This is my first time in a European city and already I feel at home here. The people I pass in the street all smile and some nod a greeting; it's really quite different from back home where strangers rarely acknowledge each other, particularly in the city.'*

He was looking in the windows of the clothing shops that he passed but most were displaying high fashion women's apparel. Martin is a tall handsome man with a shock of blonde hair neatly brushed back, and is accustomed to receiving admiring glances from women he passes in the street back in Melbourne. He found that he was receiving the same kind of looks here in Madrid and was inwardly pleased.

Further on he came to an impressive old 3 story building with the name ABC in large letters on the façade. It seemed to be filled with a variety of businesses, mostly selling clothing and accessories. An hour or so later he emerged carrying shopping bags in each hand!

He crossed over to the other side of the avenue to head back in the direction of his hotel and almost immediately saw a sign on a large palatial building announcing that this was one of the museums he had read about, the Thyssen-Bornemisza Collection.

Martin entered and asked the woman at the ticket window what kind of art they had here. As she handed him the admission ticket, she replied …. "This is an incredibly diverse collection that includes some extremely old paintings from the early days of Christianity, right through the medieval period to impressionism, post impressionism and recent contemporary art works. We are proud that virtually every well-known artist through the ages is represented in this one incredible museum."

Martin wandered through room after room enjoying this vast collection and was so engrossed that he did not realise he had been there for over 3 hours until an announcement was made that the museum was closing.

As he was strolling back to his hotel he turned over in his mind the amazing assortment of paintings he had just seen and how fantastic it must have been for the Thyssen-Bornemisza family to have travelled the world buying these treasures over a number of decades.

Collecting his room key from the front desk, he then had the porter take him and his luggage to his suite. After tipping him generously, he settled into a comfortable chair, switched on his laptop and searched for information on the museum that he had just visited. Wikipedia described how the original collection started by Baron Heinrich Thyseen-Bornemisza had been housed in the family estate at Lugarno in Northern Italy.

When the local authorities rejected the family's application to extend the property to display the ever-growing accumulation of paintings and sculptures, his son Hans moved the entire collection to Madrid where the Spanish government provided the current building in 1992. A year later, the government purchased what by then had grown into a huge collection and it has since become one of the country's most significant national museums.

By now Martin was feeling the effects of jetlag and the long walk along the Paseo Del Prado. He realised that he must have walked quite a few kilometres to and from the hotel so he lay down to catch up on some sleep before venturing out for dinner. The desk clerk had told him that the evening meal in Spain is normally taken around 9.00pm so he set the bedside alarm for

8.30 and fell exhausted onto the bed. When he awoke he was feeling somewhat peckish as it had been over 8 hours since he'd had that delicious brunch.

Not wanting to venture very far from the hotel after the afternoon's marathon walk, he chose a restaurant just across the street from the hotel's main entrance. It appeared to be very well patronised as most tables were occupied so he figured that if it was this popular, the food should be excellent.

It reminded him of the saying back in Australia, that if there are a lot of trucks parked outside a roadside café, the food must be good as truck drivers are renowned for being very fussy with their meals.

After he was seated at a small table at the rear of the restaurant, he looked around the large room and saw that many of the tables had families with children so he assumed they were probably local Spaniards who lived in the many high-rise apartments surrounding the hotel. He picked up the menu and found it was only written in Spanish. Obviously a place not geared up for tourists!

There were two men sitting at the next table and he turned to them and said, "Excuse me, if you speak English could you please help me understand the dishes on the menu?" Expecting them to be locals, he was surprised to hear an American accent when one of them replied. "No problem buddy, I am from Los Angeles and speak Spanish fluently. It's an important requirement for anyone wanting to be a police officer in Southern California. I'm Hank and my friend here is Charlie."

It turned out that they were here for the symposium on art crime and when he told them that he was also here for the same reason, they invited him to join them at their table.

They were keen to compare police operating methods in Australia with those in America. One of the major differences they discovered during their conversation was the various terminology used. For example, a sheriff in the US was the chief law officer of a county whilst in Australia, a sheriff delivers court summons and follows up on unpaid fines. Martin became so engrossed in their discussions that he was unable to recall later whether he had enjoyed the meal or not!

It was quite late by the time they finished their reminiscences about some of the cases they had been involved with and the massive increase in art crime that was now being experienced around the world. As they were staying at the same hotel, they arranged to meet again in the hotel dining room for breakfast and walk together to the Conference Centre the next day.

Before going to sleep, Martin emailed his sister to call their mother and let her know that he had arrived safely in Spain and was already settling into a routine here in Madrid. Tomorrow would be the first day of the conference and he was looking forward to it.

....

CHAPTER 4

OCTOBER 1 to 10, MADRID AND BILBAO, SPAIN

The conference was attended by more than two hundred delegates from countries as diverse as South Africa, Saudi Arabia and Brazil. These days most developed nations have museums and art galleries with large collections representing huge investments and it is important that they keep up with the best ways to ensure their treasures remain safe.

As long as there have been art collections in the world, there have been people ready to steal them and sell them to others who may not be too concerned about having the relevant internationally recognized documents proving provenance. From the earliest days of Christianity, churches had commissioned artists to paint religious scenes from the bible and centuries later these paintings, usually on wooden panels became valuable targets for thieves.

The representatives of the International Art Loss Register, based in London, opened the forum and presented facts and figures on paintings and sculptures that had never been recovered. Thefts were not only from museums but also from private collections. They estimated that world-wide, paintings valued at more than $6 billion were stolen and seldom recovered. This makes it the third largest international crime after drugs and arms smuggling.

One of the American representatives spoke at length about the long running investigation that eventually closed down the famous New York Knoedler Gallery through which some 80 million dollars of forgeries had passed, including a Jackson Pollock that had sold for many millions of dollars.

A British policeman talked about one of their most loved artists, John Constable, whose paintings were copied by a master forger named James Orrock. His reproductions were so good that some of the major galleries in the U.K. had innocently exhibited his work as genuine Constable paintings!

In Germany, an art forger had sold copies of famous paintings valued at millions of dollars including one supposed to have been by Max Ernst. It was so good it had been included in a retrospective of that artist's works at the Metropolitan Museum of Art in New York!

The team from Interpol joined in the discussion late in the morning detailing specific pieces of missing art that they had been investigating and which had come to a dead end, sometimes after years of investigation. They handed out lists of the artworks with photos attached requesting assistance from the world-wide audience filling the conference centre hall.

Throughout the ensuing week, detectives from police forces from some 55 countries presented papers on art crime in their own countries and the methods they were employing not only in tracking down the thieves, but also new security technology to help prevent theft from valuable art collections.

It was mentioned during the forum that Italy is the only country that has a special police force dedicated to protecting the nation's incredible collection of art.

Martin was one of the speakers on the third day of the conference and he explained how his department kept detailed computer records of all major art works owned by museums, galleries and major private collections throughout Australia. This had helped his department in solving almost all of the art thefts over the few past years.

During the mining boom years of the 1970's and 1980's, many of the largest corporations in Australia had purchased expensive paintings to display in their boardrooms and on management office walls.

Eventually, when the value of these collections grew to tens of millions of dollars, the decision was made to either sell them or in some cases, donate them to public galleries and museums. As more and more people joined the art market, the number of private collections grew and therefore increased the opportunities for art crime. A recent study showed that art theft had increased more than threefold since the 1970's.

A major part of Martin's presentation related to the growing number of fraud cases that were occurring with Aboriginal paintings. Some of the indigenous painters had become famous world-wide and a huge business has been created by ruthless art dealers getting some desperate Aborigines to copy the styles of the better known artists. These paintings are then sold to unsuspecting customers from overseas at greatly inflated prices.

During coffee breaks and over lunch, the delegates moved around chatting to each other and by the end of the conference, Martin had made a lot of new contacts and received invitations to visit police departments in a number of countries. He was pleased to find that English was the language used by most delegates as he had only had a few years of French lessons at high school and had never had the opportunity to use it since then.

Following the end of the symposium, he spent the weekend visiting all the best galleries and museums in Madrid, the highlight for him being a whole day spent looking at the huge collection of art treasures in the Prado.

That night he went with the two Americans to see a soccer match at the huge Santiago Bernabéu Football Stadium located in the city centre, and watched the home team Real Madrid defeat the visiting Dutch team, Feyenoord Rotterdam 3 goals to 2.

All in all, Martin felt that he had just spent one of the most interesting weeks of his life and was now looking forward to his planned vacation visiting Bilbao.

On Sunday, the hotel's travel office arranged his trip to Bilbao. They provided a first class train ticket which was to depart Madrid early Monday morning and get him into Bilbao mid-afternoon October 10. They also reserved a room in a hotel that they told him was a short walk to the Guggenheim Museum.

He spent his last evening in Madrid, dining with the two Californian police officers he had met on his first night there. He checked out of the hotel early Monday morning and took a taxi to the central railway station.

The journey was on one of Spain's fabulous high-speed trains which was luxurious and far better than any train Martin had travelled on in Australia. He had lunch in the dining car as it passed through the sensational countryside. Lush, forested mountains with scores of wind turbines standing proudly on almost every peak like *'Lords of the Manors'* surveying their kingdoms spread out before them!

Arriving at the old central station in Bilbao early afternoon, Martin stopped to admire the huge end wall of stained glass window panes that was beaming an eerie multi-coloured glow onto the faces of the passengers as they thronged past the uniformed station attendants. Martin walked out into the bright sunshine and hailed a taxi to take him to his hotel which as promised was located directly opposite the Guggenheim Museum.

Despite having relaxed for hours on the train as it meandered through the Spanish countryside and doing little else but sit and stare out of the window, Martin found that travelling is tiring and after a light meal in the hotel dining room, retired to his room.

He plugged his camera into his laptop and scrolled through the photos he had taken from the train of the spectacular scenery and was quite pleased with the results. He then sat at the desk and wrote some emails to family and colleagues back home. He had planned to start writing a report on the conference but soon found that his eyelids were drooping so decided that could wait for another day. He fell into bed and slept soundly with no idea of the adventure that awaited him the next day.

....

CHAPTER 5

BILBAO, OCTOBER 12

Martin was collected early from his hotel by a uniformed officer and driven along Calle Luis Brinas to the Bilbao Police Headquarters which is a drab looking brick building more reminiscent of an old factory than a government office. He was taken straight up to the office of Chief Inspector Segueras.

He was introduced to two detectives assigned to the team investigating the murder on the funicular and was pleased to find that they both had an excellent knowledge of English as well. The only Spanish Martin had picked up since arriving was '*buenas dias*' and '*gracias*'.

The Chief Inspector told Martin that he had called Melbourne the night before to discuss Martin's availability to assist with the murder investigation. "I spoke to the Police Commissioner, Sir Charles MacPherson and he agreed that you could stay in Bilbao as long as was reasonably needed, but this was conditional on you being eventually returned to Melbourne. He told me that you are considered a rather important asset!"

It also transpired that during the night whilst Martin was sleeping, the Bilbao coroner had carried out an autopsy on the body and found that the fingerprints matched those of a man who had often run afoul of the law. "We now know that his name is Alberto Rivera and he was 42 years old. Our records show that he had spent the last three years behind bars for aggravated assault and burglary. He had only been discharged from prison a couple of months ago.

On his release, he had found work with an industrial cleaning contractor that was well known for employing people who had previously spent time in prison."

One of the detectives took over saying, "This cleaning company has long been suspected of being involved in a number of large thefts of office equipment such as laptop computers and printers but the police have been unable to gather sufficient evidence to bring charges that would stand up in court. Their access after-hours in some of the city's most prominent businesses gave them plenty of opportunities but they seemed to have always covered their tracks well. So well in fact, that despite the police concerns, they managed to secure contracts with some of the largest corporations in Bilbao and even a few of the local government offices!"

He went on, "It appears that the dead man usually worked evenings cleaning offices and public bathrooms in a number of Bilbao's major companies. They also have contracts with a small number of organizations in nearby towns." The detectives were today questioning his supervisor over his movements during the week before he was shot. The records were being checked by the cleaning company and they were to respond later this morning with details of the places he had been instructed to clean and whether he was working alone or with others.

The detectives had set up a large pin-board to display evidence and information related to this case which unfortunately was not a lot at this time. So far they had photos of the body in the train and a mug shot of the victim taken when he was sent to prison a little over three years ago.

The lead detective, Carlos, told the group of the forensic department's interim report. "A single bullet had lodged in the man's brain and had been extracted by the coroner. It was found to be a 9mm slug with markings indicating that it had most likely been fired from a Glock 17. This type of pistol is one of the most popular hand guns in the world, and is often the choice of police in many countries."

The manager of the cleaning company called back around midday and advised that Alberto Rivera had been cleaning the administration offices of a large airfreight company called West Coast Freight Forwarders for the past two weeks. He had been accompanied each night by a woman named Rosie da Silva, a Portuguese gypsy. The addresses of both people were provided and the detectives called the woman and told her that a car would be arriving shortly to bring her to police headquarters to assist them in their enquiries into the death of one of her colleagues. Two of the team would go to the victim's place to look around and talk to neighbours. Martin was invited to accompany them and assist with the search of the man's apartment.

Alberto Rivera's home was a run-down residential building in an industrial area at the edge of town. The detectives were surprised to find that despite its dilapidated condition, the building actually employed a concierge. He was found asleep at his desk in the front office near the elevators.

The police woke him up and asked to be taken to Alberto Rivera's apartment. They told him, "Signor Rivera has passed away suddenly under unusual circumstances and because of that, we need to check out some things for the coroner."

No further explanation was offered and the concierge was obviously disinterested in the goings on surrounding the death of one of his tenants so did not argue with them.

The dead man had lived in a small apartment on the top floor of the building and the policemen had to walk up four flights of stairs because the elevator was out of order. From its unkempt condition, it looked as though it had been out of order for a very long time! Once the door to the apartment had been opened by the concierge, the detectives instructed him to return to his office downstairs.

The place was sparsely furnished and extremely untidy. There were piles of garbage all over the floor and the kitchen sink was filled with dirty dishes. The three men all donned surgical gloves and commenced searching for anything that might link Alberto Rivera to some activity that would give them a clue as to the reason for his violent death.

The senior detective, Carlos, suggested to the others, "In our experience over the past few years, crimes of this nature were usually a result of the victim being involved in some drug related dealings. Looking around his apartment, I would have to say if he was dealing in drugs he must have been small fry as there is no sign of him having lots of cash to throw around." Surprisingly for this day and age, the man did not possess a computer and no mobile phone could be found. There were no photos of family or friends on display and no notepads either in the kitchen or living room.

The only document of a personal nature found was a folder of bank statements and this was picked up to take back to headquarters for inclusion in the evidence file. They found a photo-copied sketch of the freight company's office and warehouse clearly showing the location of the Customs cage. It also detailed the locations of external doors where goods can be delivered into the building. After studying it closely, Carlos told the others, "It is obvious that he made this map for his accomplice so he could find his way around the sprawling complex."

One of the detectives found a Spanish to Russian phrase book and commented that it seemed to be an unusual selection of reading for an ex-convict who had become an office cleaner. After an hour rummaging around the apartment all three men agreed that the search had been mostly fruitless and they hoped that the questioning of neighbours might turn up something more helpful for the investigation.

Martin accompanied the two police officers as they knocked on the doors of each of the apartments in the building. Some residents were not at home but the woman in the apartment opposite the victim invited them in and was very happy to tell all she knew about her neighbour. Every apartment building has at least one *'busy-body'* and this woman was obviously the eyes and ears of all that goes on in this place!

She told them, "Because Alberto was out working each night, I would often see him around the building during the afternoon as he usually slept all morning. He rarely had visitors but over the past couple of weeks, a man had been coming to see him around the middle of the afternoon two or three times a week. He usually stayed for about an hour. I saw Alberto's visitor often enough to be able to describe him as a short dumpy man with a big mop of grey hair. I only heard him speak a couple of times as he was going into the neighbour's place when I happened to be passing in the hallway. They weren't speaking Spanish and although I sometimes watch foreign movies on TV, I wasn't able to recognise this language. It definitely wasn't English or German or French as I have a satellite dish on my balcony and I like to watch movies from those countries. I have a feeling it might have been Eastern European."

The detectives thanked her, gave her a business card with their names and a direct telephone number to their department at police headquarters. They asked her to call them immediately if she remembered anything else.

Most of the other neighbours they were able to interview could not offer any assistance as typically they generally tried to keep to themselves and not get involved with other residents in the building. The exception was one young man living down the hall. He told them, "I have a small computer repair business and work from home so apart from when I go out to pick up or return a customer's computer, I am here most of the day. During the past week or so, I had noticed a fancy car parked out the front on a number of afternoons.

What was particularly interesting to me was that the car had a chauffeur who looked like someone out of a gangster film! I had the opportunity one day as I was returning home to walk past this car and was able to get a good glimpse of the driver. He was so large, he sat hunched over the steering wheel with the top of his head actually touching the roof lining. I was also surprised to see that this big hulk of a man wore his hair tied back in a ponytail." Stopping briefly to let the detective who was taking notes catch up, he then went on.

"Being somewhat interested in cars, I am able to recognize most makes and models and I am positive that this car was a black Mercedes S500. It is definitely not the sort of vehicle we would normally expect to see in our neighbourhood" After advising him that he may be required at a later date to identify the chauffeur, they thanked him for this helpful information. The trio then headed back to police headquarters to inform the Chief Inspector of their findings and to discuss the next step in the investigation process.

When they arrived, the Chief Inspector was anxiously waiting to tell them his latest news. "Whilst you men were out in the suburbs getting the lowdown on the victim, I received a call from the director of the Guggenheim Museum to report that one of the most important paintings that was to be part of a new exhibition that was still being set up had been stolen from a freight company's warehouse! He is a good friend of mine and wanted me to attend the gala opening night which was planned for next week. Meanwhile, they will now have to change their program to exclude this painting and order new brochures from the printer. They will also have to reorganize the layout of the paintings on display." He then told me, "The exhibition was showcasing modern art from the 20th Century and the missing painting was expected to be one of the most important examples in the collection to be exhibited. It was by the late American artist Jackson Pollock, and measures approximately 300 cm x 200 cm. The director explained that the painting had only been discovered in the past year stored in a New York Long Island attic by the descendants of a deceased farmer when they were clearing out the place to sell the property.

The farmer had been a long-time friend of the artist and it was presumed Pollock had given it to his friend as payment for some favour. It was covered over with a tarpaulin and estimated to have been there for around 60 years. The painting had writing on the back naming it *'Pole of Poles'* and was assumed to be the last of his *'Poles series'*, the name no doubt a symbol of his Polish heritage. Because it did not appear in any catalogue of Pollock's works, it had been through a lengthy period of authentication before being declared to be genuine and the Guggenheim Museum had only then agreed to include it in this exhibition. As you might imagine, there had been a lot of publicity surrounding this painting in art circles around the world. It was featured in art magazines with particular emphasis on its first public showing being a coup for the Guggenheim Museum in Bilbao."

He went on, "The shock of the sudden loss of this painting will cause a delay to the exhibition opening although the rest of the museum will be open as usual for visitors to see their permanent collections and other smaller changing exhibitions. I obtained the name of the manager of the freight company, their address and telephone number. They are located in the town of Vitoria-Gastiez which is about 65kms south of Bilbao. I telephoned the manager and explained that I had heard about the robbery from the director of the Guggenheim museum and asked why he hadn't called the police before this. He replied that the crate with the painting had been sent by airfreight from New York and since arriving had been stored in a caged area where special high value items were kept until they had been cleared by the Spanish Customs Department. They are never certain when clearance might take place and in the meantime no-one had been in the area of the Customs cage for a couple of days. Because of this, they hadn't checked the crate to notice that it had been opened and the painting was missing. As things turned out, they had received a call from the Customs

Department this morning to say that their officers would be coming this afternoon to check the contents of the crate. The warehouse foreman had then gone down to the Customs cage to ensure that nothing was blocking access for the Customs officers when they arrived. It was then it was noticed that the lock had been broken on the gate and the lid of the crate with the painting had been removed! The manager then instructed the foreman to have every available person search every inch of the warehouse just in case somehow or other the painting had been removed and placed on a shelf. The search had just been completed when I telephoned. Obviously this was a very embarrassing situation for the manager and he was grasping at straws as nothing is permitted to be moved out of the cage before it has been cleared. I immediately sent two of my officers from the robbery division to the freight company to investigate the theft and they are expected back shortly."

The Chief Inspector was certain that this wasn't a matter of coincidence and there was likely to be a connection between the theft of the painting and the murder of the cleaner. He decided to combine the resources of the two police investigating teams.

Martin decided to wait a little longer before visiting the Guggenheim Museum as he definitely wanted to see the new exhibition which was going to display some of his favourite artist's works. He was extremely disappointed at the delay in opening the new exhibition as after all, going to this museum was the main reason he had come to Bilbao.

CHAPTER 6

BILBAO, OCTOBER 13

The Manager of West Coast Freight Forwarders, an American named Andrew Carter, made the meeting room at the warehouse available to enable the police to set up their investigation team. The primary task for the team from Robbery Division was to work through three days of CCTV footage that had now been provided by the freight company. Unfortunately, there were no security cameras operating inside the warehouse close to the Customs cage but there were a number of them installed at each corner of the building pointing towards the roller shutter doors as well as inside the main office area.

Whilst the team was reviewing the security videos at the warehouse, Martin and the other team sat around a table at police headquarters discussing the evidence they had collected so far. They went over the various possibilities that could lead them in the right direction to track down both the murderer and the stolen painting. They had now added to their murder investigation pin-board some photos of the stolen painting that the Museum had sent to them a few hours earlier.

Firstly, the cleaners were the obvious suspects to have removed the painting from the cage as they had access to most areas and had keys enabling them to open all office doors as well as the warehouse where they had to clean the bathrooms and toilets. This was underscored by the finding of the hand-drawn map of the warehouse at the dead man's apartment.

The Jackson Pollack painting had been removed from the shipping crate in its frame and would have required a vehicle large enough to take the 3 x 2 metre painting away.

As the truck the cleaners used was a large Mercedes Sprinter van, the detectives believed it was high enough to slide the picture in through the back doors of this type of vehicle. To be sure, the detectives would contact the local Mercedes dealer and check the dimensions.

At the same time, it would have required at least two people to handle the weight and bulk of the painting which meant that the murdered man must have let someone else in during the night. One of the detectives suggested that the cleaners would probably have been commissioned to carry out the theft by an international syndicate specializing in obtaining valuable art works on consignment for wealthy unscrupulous clients.

Martin told the group something that he had learned at the symposium the previous week. "Over the past few decades, numerous stolen art treasures have found their way into the homes of Russian, American, Chinese and South American billionaires where they can only be admired by their families and very close associates. These people usually have grand mansions with walls big enough to hang the largest paintings! It has often been extremely difficult for Interpol to follow through on leads in these countries as the wealthy pay huge sums to protect their interests from the prying eyes of the authorities. Some clients generally want only to collect the old masters such as Rubens and Carravaggio whilst others are more interested in modern artists such as in this case."

Carlos then took over to propose, "The next thing to work out is how they would get such a large picture out of the country as it was most unlikely that it would be offered to a buyer inside Spain. Apart from the state of the Spanish economy, there would be too much publicity in this country to try to hide it locally." Martin added, "In my experience, the usual way to transport a large painting is to carefully remove the canvas from the wooden frame and roll it up with a thin Mylar fabric separating the paint from the reverse side of the canvas as it is rolled. It can then be hidden in a tube that makes it easy to move around. The tube could be made from thick cardboard or a length of PVC water pipe which is light weight but solid enough to protect the painting from damage whilst in transit. I estimate that when rolled up, it would require a tube of between 200 and 250mm diameter and the size and weight would need at least two men to lift and carry it."

Carlos continued, "As the borders between all the countries in the Euro Zone are now open, there shouldn't be a problem taking it far from Spain and then sending it by ship or air freight to its ultimate destination. Passing through Customs in most other countries could present a problem but in some places, particularly those that had previously been behind the so called *'Iron Curtain'*, a little bit of monetary persuasion will ensure that the package is not opened and will continue uninhibited to its destination!"

Martin excused himself from the discussions to telephone one of the Interpol contacts he had met at the conference in Madrid the previous week. He was based at the Interpol headquarters in Paris. "We met at the recent art crime conference in Madrid and as it happens, I am still in Spain having a short vacation. As it happens, I had placed your business card in my wallet without realising at the time that I would need to refer to it so soon," he told Jean- Paul Gaumont, the Interpol contact. "I want to report the theft of a Jackson Pollock painting from a freight company's warehouse in Bilbao where I am visiting at the moment. It was to be included in a forthcoming exhibition at the Guggenheim Museum. I will be emailing through photos of the painting in the next half hour to the address on your business card."

Jean-Paul whose English was impeccable, replied, "Nice to hear from you so soon after we met, but sorry it's about such an incredible theft of a painting destined for an exhibition at such a famous museum. Interpol will spread the word quickly to our operatives around the world to watch and listen for any news of this painting." Martin then went on to tell him briefly of the murder he had witnessed and that is the reason he is now assisting the Bilbao police with their investigation.

The team watching the security videos were getting bored after hours of monotonous viewing seeing nothing suspicious and were about to take a break when one of them spotted something that didn't look quite right.

The cleaner's truck had backed up to one of the large loading bay roller doors and a shadowy figure hopped out and disappeared inside. The CCTV picture was too fuzzy due to the blackness of the night and the scarcity of lighting in that area to enable obtaining a good description of the person. It was noted that it was a short grey-haired man who appeared to have a limp. This scene was marked for copying and sending to their high-tech electronic forensic department where they would try to improve the quality and get a better look at the furtive figure disappearing into the warehouse.

Half an hour later on the same video, two men came out carrying bags of garbage which were dropped in the waste bins nearby and then went back into the warehouse.

Because the back of the truck was virtually inside the doorway of the loading dock, it was not possible from where the CCTV camera was located, to see anything being placed into the truck. Soon after, one man got into the truck and it drove away whilst the other man went back into the warehouse.

Once again, this section of the video was also marked to go with the other one to the electronics specialists in the IT department at police headquarters for improvement of the picture quality.

Back at headquarters, Chief Inspector Segueras came by to inform the team about a telephone call he had received from the Biscay Provincial President and the Bilbao mayor. "Despite the economic downturn which has driven Spain into difficult times over the past few years, we have been instructed to treat this case with the utmost urgency. I have also been assured that money would be made available to cover whatever costs are needed to bring the perpetrators to justice and to get the stolen painting returned so it can be included in the exhibition at the Guggenheim Museum as soon as possible. Obviously, the apprehension of the murderer of the cleaner is also to be given high priority."

The Chief Inspector continued, "Our local government is extremely embarrassed by what has happened and believe their lucrative tourism industry could be seriously affected by negative reporting of the recent events. The Provincial President also told me that it was his intention to keep the Federal Government in Madrid up to date on the progress of the investigation. He believed they could also get involved if the case was not solved promptly."

As it was now late in the day, the Chief Inspector told his men to head home for some well-earned rest and to return fresh tomorrow to really knuckle down and hunt for clues. He then invited Martin to dine with him that evening at his home to meet his wife and family.

He picked Martin up from his hotel at 8.00 and drove him out to his home which was in a new housing estate to the east of the city. On the way, he suggested to Martin that he call him José when they were away from headquarters. When they arrived at the house, Martin's first impression was of a spectacular front garden, manicured lawns, topiaried shrubs and rows of beautiful rose bushes.

It turned out that Señor Segueras was an avid gardener and each weekend this was his way of unwinding from the pressures of his duties as the most senior police officer in Northern Spain. Set back from the garden was a large modern double storey home with floor to ceiling windows in front through which the family could sit and admire the garden.

After being introduced to his wife Marianna and their three children, Martin and the Chief settled down in the lounge where pre-dinner cocktails were served from a large built-in bar. He was fascinated to learn to the children whose ages ranged from seven to thirteen were being taught to speak 3 languages other than Spanish, French, German and English. José explained, "It is very important these days for young people entering the workforce to be able to converse in the most used languages whether for commerce, medical studies or IT." Martin replied, "Unfortunately, Australians are similar to the Americans in that they feel the rest of the world should speak English! Although all schools offer classes in different languages, it would be rare for the graduating students to continue learning and using another language once they head for university."

Whilst Señora Segueras went to the kitchen to finalize dinner, Martin discussed his early training and subsequent elevation within the Victorian Police Force and described a little of what the average lifestyle was like in Australia. He told him, "Although, I have only been in Spain for a short time, I have the feeling that in many respects, family life here is not so different from ours.

Some things I have noticed that are different is the shops closing for afternoon siesta and the late meal times, especially your evening dinner which is much later than ours. At home, people tend to sit down for the evening meal between 6.30 and 7.00. None-the-less, I have quickly adjusted to these changes and am quite enjoying it all."

The Chief had invited a niece to join them for dinner and she turned out to be a raven haired beauty named Isabella who spoke English with very little accent. She explained to Martin, "After graduating with a law degree from the Bilbao Campus of the Basque University, I spent a few years travelling the world and gathered valuable experience working in England, Canada and the U.S.A."

She continued her story, "My last work experience position was with a large law firm in Los Angeles which I enjoyed very much. I was involved in some very interesting white collar crime lawsuits and the verdicts often resulted in enormous payouts for the victims. The law firm's commission was also substantial and I received some excellent bonuses which enabled me to travel back to Spain the long way round.

I flew across the Pacific Ocean to New Zealand for a brief stopover where I went skiing in the beautiful South Island, then

I had two weeks in Australia joining a tour across the *'Top End'* that travelled from Darwin to Broome through the spectacular Kimberley region. That scenery was like nothing I had seen anywhere else on my travels, it was absolutely amazing. When we were staying in the Kakadu National Park, we were taken one day to see Aboriginal paintings on huge rocks that were tens of thousands of years old. They depicted scenes of animals and people which recorded the life they led all those years ago. These amazing examples of primitive art reminded me of the cave paintings we have here in the north of Spain. They were discovered in 1880 and the cave is now a UNESCO Heritage Site. It is called the Cave of Altamira and is outside the small town of Santillana Del Mar, just 30kms from Santander which is the next city west of Bilbao along the coast."

She had returned to Bilbao to take up a position with one of the leading law firms in the area. Isabella handed Martin a business card and suggested he call her when he had a free evening so she could show him around the city and told him that if he was still in Bilbao next weekend, she would like to take him to see the paintings in the Cave of Altamira.

After a delightful meal, they sat in the lounge and Martin was questioned about life in Melbourne. He told them it was a sprawling metropolis with a population of more than four million people mostly living in suburban detached houses.

"Many of my neighbours have swimming pools and tennis courts as Australians generally love the outdoors." Marianna, who also spoke excellent English asked, "Is it true that Australia consider itself to be a truly multi-cultural society?" Martin replied, "These days, the country has an amazing mix of nationalities and cultures possibly unmatched by any other place in the world and Melbourne reflects this with its incredible diverse society."

Martin continued, "It has developed from a country of indigenous Aboriginal tribes to a faraway land colonised with convicts by the British in the eighteenth century to a country that has for the past 100 years accepted immigrants escaping from terrible conflicts and natural disasters all around the world. There was a shameful period when the government in the early part of the 20th century instigated what was known as *'The White Australia Policy'* which prevented emigration of people from non-European backgrounds. Fortunately, this policy was buried long ago together with the politicians that dreamt it up and the doors were thrown open to a huge influx of migrants from all over Asia, Africa, South America and the Middle East."

Marianna then asked Martin how this relaxed immigration policy was viewed by the old establishment and what affect it has had on daily life in Australia. He replied, "Until the end of the Second World War, the majority of movies shown in our cinemas were from Britain or America. In the 1950s a huge number of immigrants were brought in from Europe, many from Italy and Greece and with them came a flood of Mediterranean style restaurants, movies in their languages, and radio stations started including music and news broadcasts from those countries.

"Soon after came the Korean War and when that ended many South Koreans moved to Sydney bringing their culture to that city. In the late 60s and early 70s, boatloads of people flooded into Australia from Vietnam, the majority finishing up in Melbourne. Their influence can be seen all around the city with some areas in particular filled with Vietnamese restaurants and food shops. Australia is now very cosmopolitan and Melbourne in particular is the multi-cultural capital of the country."

After a sip of wine, Martin continued… "From the 1990's, the main source of immigration has been from desperate people escaping the wars in the Middle East and Afghanistan as well as African nations such as The Sudan. Instead of waiting for formal immigration permits which can take a long time, the majority of these immigrants found their way to Indonesia where they paid great sums of money to board rusty unseaworthy boats to try and enter Australia illegally on the north coast of our largest state, Western Australia.

Many boats sank and thousands drowned. On one hand, we can understand the people wishing to escape the horrors taking place in their homelands and head for a safer place to live, but unfortunately they were being exploited by so called *'people smugglers'*. Because of their desperate circumstances they were willing to try any means even if it was extremely risky.

The flood of so-called *'boat people'* has abated recently due to co-operation between the Indonesian and Australian governments but the problem hasn't gone away. Europe has also experienced being inundated with immigrants escaping the horrors of war in the Middle East and North Africa. Similar to the way desperate people were trying to get to Australia, thousands have drowned when leaking boats sank in the Mediterranean between African and Italy."

Isabella joined in saying, "Here in Spain, we have also been facing large numbers of immigrants from North Africa, particularly from Morocco which is so very close to Southern Spain. The situation has been made more difficult because Spain has been going through tough economic times for some years now and there is very little work available for these immigrants. This has resulted in a huge increase in crime, particularly violent robberies. It's not so bad in this part of the country but according to my uncle José along the Mediterranean coast and in the city of Madrid, it's a major cause of concern for the police in those areas."

Martin asked, "Do you have a lot of new Mosques to cater for these immigrants? In Melbourne they have sprung up mostly in the outer suburbs. This has been a shock for some of the older people who are more used to seeing churches on every corner!"

Isabella answered, "Not around here, but further south there are plenty. Remember when the Moors ruled Spain they built some magnificent Mosques around the country and then after the Muslims were deported, the Spanish Royal Family headed by my namesake, Queen Isabella the first and her husband Ferdinand decreed that all mosques were to be converted into Catholic cathedrals. One of the most amazing of these is the

Mezguita in Cordoba and if I get a chance to see you again while you are here, I'll bring a book which shows photos of this transition from Islam to Catholicism."

Having had a delightful evening with this lovely family, Martin thanked Marianna and José Segueras and told Isabella that he hoped they could meet again while he was in Bilbao.

The Chief then drove Martin back to his hotel and on the way they discussed ideas about the next steps for hunting down the murderer and thieves. He said, "Although we are absolutely certain of the connection between both crimes, we have nothing definite to go on which would enable us to proceed further." Martin replied, "The description they were given of the chauffeur in the Mercedes was similar to that I gave of the killer on the train." José tried to be more optimistic in his reply, "Hopefully, the forensic team will give us a break-through on the identity of the other man seen in the CCTV footage and Interpol might be able to give us some leads on who would be interested in a stolen Jackson Pollock painting."

They bid each other good night and Martin sat in his hotel room for quite a while emailing friends and colleagues of the latest events.

∙∙∙∙∙∙∙∙∙∙∙∙∙∙∙∙∙∙∙∙∙∙∙∙∙∙∙∙∙∙

CHAPTER 7

BILBAO, OCTOBER 14

Back in the Crime Investigation Room at Police Headquarters the next day, the two teams started sifting through all of the known facts about both events.

Carlos stood in front of the pin-board and spoke to the assembled team. "Firstly, the murdered cleaner who had been working at the West Coast Freight Forwarders has a long history as a thief and was obviously chosen for his criminal background. He had been in and out of prison since he was a teenager, mostly for petty theft. His current job allowed him access to the warehouse at night which would have been a perfect choice for whoever was masterminding the robbery. Having recently been released from prison and obviously short of cash, it would have been easy to sign him up for a straightforward job like smashing a padlock and removing a painting from a wooden crate. He no doubt had been offered an attractive amount of cash and this would have meant that it would have made it an easy decision for him to accept."

Carlos went on, "The reason for his murder may have been because he had demanded more money after the theft had been carried out successfully or possibly because the people behind the job had always intended to dispose of any potential weak links.

They probably didn't expect that we would trace his identity as quickly as we did but in today's world, with almost everyone on the planet catalogued in someone's data base, there's a very good chance that identification can be achieved extremely fast as was the case here."

One of the other officers then stood up and said, "We have now checked the victim's account with the Bank of Santander which showed a number of consecutive cash deposits of between 2000 and 3000 euros over the previous 2 weeks which totalled 10,000 euros. As his salary as a cleaner was only 350 euros a week, these large deposits could only have come from some illegal source and would have been a real bonanza for someone in the cleaner's financial situation."

Another of the team then suggested, "He didn't live in the suburbs above Bilbao where one would ride the funicular to work so he must have been lured there with a promise of a further cash payment for the express purpose to murder him."

Martin then stood up and addressed the group... "The Jackson Pollock painting would have been a very unusual choice for some art collector to request. A short while ago, I spoke with the director of the Guggenheim Museum who told me that when this painting first appeared earlier this year, everyone in the art world was shocked and disbelieving. Those that had followed the career of this artist over the decades publicly declared it to be a fake. Jackson Pollock died in 1956 in a car crash on New York's Long Island not far from where he lived and had his studio. It was previously thought that every one of his paintings had been accounted for and catalogued.

For a painting as large as this to be suddenly found was initially thought to be highly suspicious especially as there had been a number of counterfeit Jackson Pollock paintings found in the USA a few years ago. It was only after extensive research by experts and its subsequent authentication, did the Guggenheim Museum agree to include it in this new exhibition. Up to this time, very few people had even laid eyes upon it."

Martin paused briefly for a drink of water before continuing... "Naturally, people who are interested in art would have read about it in any of a number of glossy art magazines published monthly and circulated around the world. I did some research on line last night and found that its potential value has not yet been precisely established. This is because it has not yet changed hands at auction where the public's opinion is realistically determined. Despite this, I am able to offer the following relevant information. Back in 1973, the Australian Government shocked the nation by purchasing a Jackson Pollock painting for the National Gallery of Australia in Canberra. The painting is called *'Blue Poles'* and at that time they paid a world record price for a Pollock painting of 1.3 million dollars. The Australian public was outraged that such a large amount of taxpayer's money was *'wasted'* on what was widely considered a messy piece of art. Today it has been valued at more than 100 million dollars."

This revelation shocked the teams of detectives sitting around the crime room and resulted in a more determined effort to solve the mystery. Martin concluded by saying, "Obviously, the asking price for a stolen painting without any provenance would have to be substantially less but would still be in the millions. One thing that puzzles me is how did this person know which freight company was bringing the Jackson Pollock painting to Spain?" One of the officers who had been to the freight company's warehouse that morning stood up and said, "After we had seen the size of the shipping crate we asked the manager what kind of aircraft could handle something that size. He told us that they had contracted with the Russian company that hires out a fleet of the world's largest aeroplanes, including the Antonov 124. These enormous planes travel all over the world transporting equipment that is too large for other airfreight companies to handle."

A representative from the forensic IT division came by to bring them some grainy photographs of the unknown person that they had managed to produce from the CCTV footage recorded on the night of the theft. He appeared to have a thick crop of grey hair and was definitely on the short side.

This matched the description of the person that had been visiting Alberto Rivera a number of times given by the neighbour of the murdered man. Just then, the receptionist called to say Rosie da Silva, the woman who was the other cleaner on duty the night the painting was stolen, had arrived downstairs. One of the detectives went down and brought her up for questioning. Rosie turned out to be a dark haired, dark eyed young woman possibly in her mid-thirties who spoke a kind of dialect gypsy language mixing some Spanish with Portuguese and something else unknown to most of those in the room. One of the detectives offered to act as interpreter as he had had some experience dealing with many of the local gypsies often involved in petty theft. She was able to explain that on the night in question, Alberto was particularly aloof which was most unusual. He was normally chatty and pleased to have someone to talk with as he apparently led a somewhat lonely existence.

She told the team, "Alberto seemed to be able to understand her language better than most of the other people she met on the job. He had told her previously that whilst in prison, he had met people from all over Europe and had learnt to converse in a number of languages including her Gypsy language, Italian, French, English and Russian." She became nervous and asked if she could have a cigarette. They told her that smoking was not allowed in public buildings but if it would help to ease her nervousness, they could bring her a strong cup of coffee.

She thanked them and continued, "Alberto appeared to have his mind elsewhere whenever I spoke to him and he was constantly looking over my shoulder as if he was watching out for someone. For a few hours, we worked in different parts of the office and so I did not see him for quite a while, probably not until the early hours of the morning. Then I heard the big doors opening at the main loading dock and saw the cleaning van backed up against the dock platform."

She paused when one of the detectives brought her the cup of coffee and after gulping it down, she continued, "A man I had never seen before came around to the back and opened both the van doors and lifted out one of the portable vacuum cleaners and a floor scrubber that are always carried in the van. None of these events gave me any sense of anything being amiss, but then suddenly Alberto appeared and when he saw I was standing watching, came over and asked if I would help him out. He had run short of time to clean one of the offices at the rear of the building that was on his list. He gave me a 50 Euro note which I accepted gratefully and took off to attend to cleaning that particular office."

The detectives showed her the poor quality photographs that forensics had produced and asked her if this was the man. She looked closely and slowly nodded her head, saying it was difficult to be sure but the mop of grey hair definitely looked the same.

One of the detectives then asked if she had heard Alberto talking to the stranger and if so, had they been speaking Spanish.

She replied that she had heard a few words only but it didn't seem to be any language she was familiar with. The detective was on a roll then and asked if she had heard words like *'da' and 'nyet'* and her dark eyes sparkled as she replied, "Yes that was it!" They thanked her very much and arranged for a police driver to take her home.

At last, a real break-through! They stopped to have some lunch in the police canteen and whilst he was enjoying a refreshing cool salad, Martin was amazed to see that wine and low alcohol beer were available, something that definitely wouldn't be allowed in the Melbourne police headquarters! Then it was back to the crime room for some action on the latest developments. They logged on to the Spanish Immigration Department website and searched for recent arrivals of men on Russian passports. They tried a variety of dates ranging from 1 to 4 weeks prior to the theft and a long list of names was presented. They then narrowed it down with a basic description including hair colour and an estimated height.

This reduced the list to about 30 men. Spain, like many Western countries nowadays, retains photographs of all people entering the country. They were able to print out pictures of all 30 possibilities.

Two of the detectives compared the photographs with those of the man that had been videoed leaving with the van and bingo....one of these matched! A quick call to their colleagues in the Immigration Department quickly confirmed that this person had entered Spain via Madrid 3 weeks ago but had flown out yesterday from Bilbao on Air France flight 5961 at 13.25 arriving in Paris at 15.00.

His name was Alexei Nagormy and his entry card handed to immigration when he arrived in Spain stated that he was an importer and exporter of antiques and collectable art. He appears to have proven that this was indeed his chosen profession!

They then inquired if he had checked in any large item as excess baggage and they were told that they would have to inquire with the airline and get back to the police as soon as they had an answer. This could take until tomorrow as information regarding luggage and freight consignments may not be immediately available from the airline.

Carlos exclaimed, "Martin, this could be the answer to your question about how the perpetrator knew where the painting would be before it was delivered to the museum. Assuming he is our man, Alexei Nagormy must have had connections with the Russian airfreight company and been able to track the painting's movement from the USA."

Martin by now was feeling quite at home in Bilbao and getting to know his way around. He rode one of the sleek tramcars back to his hotel where he decided to dine but not before he enjoyed a long soak in the bath where he sat gazing across at the Guggenheim Museum. Although the museum was the reason he had come to Bilbao, the recent events had prevented him from being able to explore it! Hopefully one day soon, he would be able to wander through this gleaming edifice and at least examine the permanent collection of modern art.

....

CHAPTER 8

BILBAO, OCTOBER 15

On Thursday morning, Carlos, the detective in charge of the investigation addressed the men working on the case.

"As it is now certain that the mastermind, Alexei Nagormy, has departed Bilbao and by now would be safely back in Russia, our immediate attention should be focussed on the murderer in case he is still in Spain and particularly, in this area."

Together with the brief description they had from Martin and the computer repair man at the dead man's apartment building as well as some poor quality pictures taken from the CCTV camera at the exit of the Funicular, they had their *'Identikit'* specialist produce a picture of what the killer may look like. The detectives all agreed that he was probably a hired assassin and because of Martin's suggestion that the dark patches he saw on the back of the man's hands were most likely tattoos, they were leaning toward looking into members of a local bikie gang. It was no secret that many of the gang members had served time in prison for a number of major offences including possession and trafficking of drugs, armed robberies and shootings.

Amongst the local bikie gangs, one of the most notorious and with the largest membership was a group called *'Los Bandidos España'*. It had affiliations with similar clubs in Britain, the USA, Mexico, Germany, Russia and even Australia. It was decided that this would be a good place to start.

Amazingly, a check of the *'Bandidos'* website showed that their weekly members gathering happened to be scheduled for tonight at 7.30 in their club rooms. The address showed that it was located in what had once been a Customs warehouse in the old docks along the Cadagua River.

Because of the dangerous nature of this mission, showing up uninvited to a meeting of a gang of such notoriety, the Chief Inspector was called in to give permission. "I will arrange for a support group from the drug squad to accompany you together with their dogs. I believe the dogs could be extremely useful in the kind of situation I expect that you will be confronted with tonight. Not only will the dogs sniff out any drugs on the premises, they will help keep the bikies at bay."

Around 8 o'clock that evening, some 10 police, including detectives and uniformed men drove up and parked quietly near the club building. After first placing armed officers at each doorway on all sides of the building, the drug squad with their dogs entered through the front door and shouted that it was a raid. Leather jacketed bearded men ran towards the other doors only to find their paths blocked by the uniformed police pointing semi-automatic weapons at them.

All the members were lined up against the walls and searched. A number of them were found in possession of hand guns and some had boxes of pills which appeared to be amphetamines.

Once the uniformed police had secured the building and its occupants, the detectives and Martin walked along the line looking at the men and comparing the faces with the *'Identikit'* picture. Two men were selected that had similar features and not surprisingly, both had beards and tattoos on their hands!

They were hand-cuffed and led out to the waiting police cars to be taken to headquarters for questioning. Meanwhile, the drug squad arrested a number of other people who were also loaded into vans and taken into custody to be charged with firearms and drug offences.

Back at headquarters, the two men brought in for questioning over the death of the cleaner on the Funicular were fingerprinted, photographed and taken to two separate interview rooms.

Martin sat in a room that had one way windows looking into both of the interview rooms and watched the interrogations taking place. One of the investigating team sitting in the room with Martin translated what was being said. After an hour of questioning, one of the men was released as he had a bullet-proof alibi for the day of the murder....he was in a police cell having been picked up for being drunk and disorderly that morning, and had been kept locked up all day and released that night after he had sobered up!

This gave Martin a chance to concentrate on the face of the remaining suspect and the more he studied him, the more certain he was that this was the person he saw. When he told one of the other detectives that he was sure that this was the killer, a note was sent into the interrogating officer advising of this. The suspect was then told that he had been identified as the person who was alleged to have shot the cleaner on the Funicular on October 11 and would be held in custody whilst further investigations were carried out. He claimed he was innocent and that the police were only picking on him because he was a member of a bikie gang.

Whilst this was going on, forensic police were checking his fingerprints with those taken in the compartment on the train. He did not have a gun when searched at the Bandidos' clubhouse and the police believed the murder weapon would most likely have been disposed of the same day, probably now resting in mud at the bottom of the river.

The team decided it was time for a break as it had been quite a long and eventful day and everyone was exhausted. The Chief Inspector recommended that they have the weekend off and meet next on Monday morning bright and early.

Martin decided to grab a taxi back to the hotel and after sending some emails to family and friends as well as one to update the Commissioner on the latest events, he sat down and concentrated on writing his report on the Madrid conference.

He sat at his laptop typing away until well into the early hours of the morning before his eyelids drooped and he fell exhausted into bed.

....

CHAPTER 9

BILBAO, OCTOBER 16 & 17

Being Saturday, Martin was able to sleep late as the hotel maids did not bother guests until later in the morning.

After a leisurely breakfast, he walked to the Bilbao Museum which was originally the only public building in the city displaying Spanish art. It was just a 5 minute stroll from the hotel. This old museum has a large collection of Spanish Masters, particularly by Basque painters and Martin considered the paintings extremely interesting as they depicted the history of the area.

He found himself in discussion with one of the Museum attendants over a cup of coffee in the museum café about the Picasso painting *'Guernica'*. The man reiterated what Martin had heard from the barman on his first day in Bilbao. "That painting reflects such an important event in the history of this region it should be hanging here in this museum, not in Madrid." The locals obviously felt very strongly about this and had been trying for years to get it relocated here. They also discussed the recent theft of the Jackson Pollock painting from the freight company's warehouse that was destined for the new exhibition at the Guggenheim Museum. The attendant remarked, "Our local officials are very upset as this reflects badly on them and something like this will bring unwanted publicity upon Bilbao."

Martin did not tell him of his involvement but replied, "I am sure the Bilbao police will be doing everything possible to catch the thief and return the painting so it can displayed at the museum very soon."

Walking back towards the hotel along the river, Martin found himself suddenly drenched by a water installation which had myriad small jets set in the patterned brick paving. As the spray pattern of the water continually changes and the pressure increases or decreases, it often wets a large area where people are walking, thereby sprinkling them with a fine mist. It is virtually impossible to try and out-manoeuvre the sprays as you can never guess which way they will turn next. People strolling through the parkland close to the Guggenheim Museum just accept it and continue on their way with clothes a little damper than when they started out that day!

Martin sat on a nearby bench in the sun to dry off and watched children running in and out of the fountains as they danced around performing a kind of water ballet.

It was then that he noticed people going into the Guggenheim Museum and realised that this was probably a good opportunity for him to visit there as well. Somewhat excitedly, he headed for the main entrance and paid the admission fee. He was handed a map and started to wander through the variety of galleries within the museum. The interior is absolutely spectacular, and at first he was more interested in the complex construction of the lofty structures which form the supports for the titanium cladding and the stunning views of the river flowing past the huge windows.

Today he was a typical wide-eyed tourist and found himself smiling.... at last, he was able to do what he had come all this way to experience!

He walked out onto the paved deck along the river to look at the building from that side and was startled to see a huge sculpture of a spider! He wondered if it was there to welcome visitors arriving by boat and if so, would they find it an inviting subject or might it turn them away?

Eventually, he managed to actually study the art on show in the permanent collection galleries then enquired at the reception desk if the new special exhibition was now open to the public. The receptionist told him that it had opened this morning for preview only for representatives of the Press and some local Government officials. The official opening would take place next week. He told her that he was a visiting police officer from Australia who was currently assigned to the Bilbao police as part of the team investigating the theft of the Jackson Pollock painting. "It is likely I could be on my way back to Australia before the exhibition is open to the public," he told her. She asked Martin to wait a moment while she conferred with the Museum Director to check if he might be permitted to take a look at the exhibition. She suggested that he wait in the café as it might take a few minutes to contact the director who was showing the mayor and some other officials around the exhibition. Martin was enjoying a hot glass of latte when the girl found him and handed him a special pass that would allow him entry to the exhibition.

After thanking her he finished his drink and headed straight for the special exhibition hall. As it was not crowded, he had plenty of time to wander around and enjoy the art on display.

There were lots of huge paintings from American artists such as Andy Warhol, Roy Lichtenstein, Willem de Kooning, Mark Rothko, Frans Kline and Robert Rauschenberg. At the end of the room was a large space where the Jackson Pollock painting was meant to have been hanging but instead there was a sign on the wall in Spanish and English advising that the painting was temporarily unavailable for display!

As Martin wandered around the Guggenheim Museum, his mind kept returning to the robbery and the brazenness of the thieves. They had planned the theft like a military operation enabling them to remove the painting from a locked Customs cage in what should have been a very secure location in a freight company's warehouse. Having the truck backed right into the loading dock was an excellent way to prevent the cameras recording what was being put into the rear of the van.

He was also convinced that this Alexei character was the mastermind behind the theft and knew that although he wasn't the person who pulled the trigger and shot the cleaner on the funicular, the killing would have been carried out on his orders. As in a military operation, Alexei would be the general and the killer was just one of the foot soldiers. He felt pleased that they had now arrested a murder suspect who matched the description that Martin had given the police.

Martin spent Sunday morning working on his symposium report and returned to the Guggenheim Museum in the afternoon to look at the other exhibitions that were currently on show. He was enjoying the break from the intense atmosphere inside the special investigation room at the Bilbao Police Headquarters where he had spent much of the past week. It was more like being at home working rather than being on vacation.

CHAPTER 10

BILBAO, OCTOBER 18

Monday morning, bright and early, Martin arrived at Police Headquarters having by now felt confident enough to use public transport to travel to and from the hotel. He had even picked up a few more Spanish words on the way!

On arrival in the investigation room, one of the team who had spent a lot of time with Martin the previous week, took him aside and excitedly told him, "We have received an email from Air France confirming that the Russian passenger, Alexei Nagormy had checked in an excess baggage item that was placed in the freight compartment of the plane. It was a 2 metre long plastic pipe with both ends sealed, just like you suggested." He went on, "The paperwork accompanying the package stated that it contained an antique Moroccan rug. There was no reason for such an item to arouse suspicion by anyone at the airline as rugs are often transported this way. The sniffer dogs that checked packages for drugs and explosives had not raised an alarm so the contents of the plastic pipe were not checked. As it had been consigned through to Moscow, it never left the Paris airport and in fact had been on an Aeroflot flight to Russia that same evening."

Martin had been provided with a desk to work at and a PC with an internet connection. He was checking his emails; mostly from colleagues back home all tossing ideas at him that they thought might be helpful when he noticed one from the Interpol contact in Paris. Their operatives in other countries have advised that there were some rumours going around that a billionaire, possibly in South America, the U.S. or Australia had put feelers out for a rare modern painting to fill a large wall in his newly completed mansion. This person wasn't fussed who the artist might be as long as he was famous and the painting was valuable. In the early days of emails, most addresses ended in a code that signified the country where the email originated. For some time now, the majority of addresses end in *'dot com'* or *'dot org'* and could have been sent from anywhere on the planet! Although China in recent years has been buying real estate, mineral resources and agricultural businesses around the world, they hadn't yet become a major player in buying modern art of the Western World.

A meeting was called by the Chief Inspector to catch up on the progress of the investigation and he announced to Martin that following the arrest of the suspected killer, the Spanish government had decided to pay for Martin's hotel and meals whilst he was assisting them. This was a very pleasant surprise for Martin as he had only yesterday evening checked his credit card balance on-line and realised that being on an extended vacation like this was pushing his expenditures towards the limit on his card.

They filled the chief in on the movements of the Russian and the apparent relocation of the stolen painting to Moscow. The Chief Inspector responded, "I want you to immediately advise Interpol of the likelihood that the painting was now somewhere in Russia, most likely Moscow, and ask them to have their operatives follow up as soon as possible.

If necessary, we will send people to Moscow and work with Interpol to try to track down the painting. After all it shouldn't be too difficult to find Alexei Nagormy and his place of business." He went on, "I suggest that a Russian oligarch might be the ultimate purchaser as there are a large number of billionaires now in that country with plenty of money to spend on items such as expensive paintings. Artwork has proven to be an excellent investment, especially at a time in Russia when the rouble is at its lowest value in years."

Martin didn't agree with this hypothesis and said, "The message I received from Interpol quoted three countries which did not include Russia. They felt that Alexei's ultimate goal was to sell the painting to someone located in a country far from Russia. Since the sudden downturn in the oil price, the rouble has crashed making it very difficult for everyone in Russia, including oligarchs to buy goods in US dollars or Euros."

Chief Inspector Segueras went on to say, "Further to my earlier discussions with the Federal Government regarding the stolen painting, I have now informed them of the Russian connection. Because of the seriousness of the situation we now find ourselves involved in, I have requested a meeting with the Police Minister. He has arranged to fly from Madrid to Bilbao today.

He is expected to arrive at Police Headquarters in time for lunch around two o'clock. The entire team, including our Australian colleague Martin Taylor, will have lunch with us and we'll provide the Minister with as much relevant information as we can put together at this time. The Minister was surprised to hear that we had an Australian police officer working with us on the case and I explained to him in detail how this came to be."

The team working on the stolen painting was to talk again with the contact at Interpol and to obtain as much information on Alexei Nagormy and his business as was available. Martin remembered that he had briefly met a Russian Senior Police Officer based in Moscow at the Madrid conference. He told the team, "I'll zip back to my hotel and search through the collection of business cards I accumulated during the week of the conference and return with the contact details as soon as I can."

A uniformed officer was made available to take Martin to his hotel which would ensure he was back in time to meet the Police Minister. Back at the hotel, he went through more than 30 cards before finding the Russian one he was looking for. The policeman's name was Vladimir Sushkin and he was the Chief Inspector of the Moscow Fraud Squad. From all Martin had heard about Russia, this would be a very busy department!

Taking the card back with him to police headquarters, Martin showed it to his colleagues and asked, "Are any of the team conversant in Russian because I remember that in the short conversation I had with him at the Madrid conference, Inspector Sushkin was not proficient in English and it would be doubtful if he spoke any Spanish."

Carlos, the team leader who had been with Martin when they were at the victim's apartment building said, "I learnt Russian during my last two years at High School and can still remember enough of the language to hold a simple conversation. In my experience, German has usually been the common language used when we've been dealing with Russians in the past, and as it happens, I am also fluent in German having got top marks in that subject at my graduation. In Europe, it is not unusual for students to take on a number of languages and I can speak five at a reasonable level and the sixth one at conversation level only. They are, Spanish, Portuguese, Italian, English, German and some Russian."

Noting that there is a 2 hour time difference between Bilbao and Moscow, they placed a call to the Moscow police headquarters around midday. After introducing himself as a Spanish Senior Detective with the Bilbao Police Department, Carlos managed to ask in Russian to speak with Inspector Sushkin about a serious matter involving a Russian citizen.

When he came on the line, Carlos asked the Moscow police chief if he agreed to the call now being transferred onto a conference telephone as there were other police officers involved that did not speak Russian. He would assist in interpreting when needed.

Martin then joined the conversation and told Inspector Sushkin that they had met at the Madrid Conference and he was now assisting the Spanish police regarding the theft of a painting from a freight company's warehouse that was destined for a special exhibition at the Guggenheim Museum in Bilbao.

He replied in broken English, "I have read of the theft in Pravda and would be pleased to help if I can." When told of the evidence pointing to the mastermind being a certain Alexei Nagormy, Vladimir Sushkin suddenly became a little stand-offish. Martin asked if there was a problem and he replied, "You would not be familiar with how things work in Russia, but I can tell you that Mr. Alexei Nagormy has connections with a number of officials in very high places in our government."

Although he had told them his English was not perfect, there were moments when he was able to convey what he wanted to explain very well. He went on to say, "One has to tread very carefully in Russia under such circumstances. Even though our President has many times promised to stamp out the rampant corruption and fraud that had developed throughout the country under the old communist regime, things have not improved greatly."

Breaking into Russian, and with Carlos interpreting for Martin and the others, he said, "Despite the demise of communism, many of the old ways persist and it is still extremely important to have connections in high places, especially if one wants to flout the law and expect to get away with it. I suggest that the Spanish police send someone to meet with me in Moscow rather than try to work with telephone calls and emails from afar which are likely to be monitored by the authorities."

Martin thanked him and said, "We appreciate your cooperation and will get back to you shortly if the Bilbao police are granted permission to send someone to Moscow to meet with you. Meanwhile Vladimir, it would be greatly appreciated if you could do some digging around on the current business dealings of the suspect. By the way, Interpol has also been requested to make discrete inquiries regarding the same investigation so you might run across one or more of their operatives in Moscow asking questions about a large painting stolen from Spain. Any assistance you can give will help us in our efforts towards catching the thief."

About 1.30 in the afternoon, Chief Inspector Segueras appeared in the crime investigation room with a distinguished looking gentleman who was introduced as the Federal Police Minister, Don José Miguel Carreras.

They sat around a large table which was littered with sheets of paper and photographs all pertaining to the two investigations related to the murder and the theft. Large plates of sandwiches and bowls of salads were brought in and handed around so they could eat lunch whilst the meeting took place.

The Minister's knowledge of English was reasonable but limited so the meeting was conducted in Spanish with Carlos once again taking the role of interpreter, this time translating the Minister's questions on the main points for Martin.

After the two crimes had been clearly explained to the Minister and the results of the investigation so far detailed, the Chief Inspector proudly announced, "I am pleased to tell you that permission has been given for two of the team to travel to Moscow to follow up and hopefully solve one of the largest and most brazen thefts in Spanish history."

After a pause, he continued, "The Spanish government has been particularly embarrassed by the enormity of this theft and is determined to solve the case and get the painting back so it can go on display at the Guggenheim Museum as soon as possible."

It had been decided that Carlos and Martin should be the two to go and their passports would be couriered immediately to the Russian Consulate to obtain visas.

Martin's head was spinning at having been selected for the mission to Russia and he thanked the Chief and the Minister for their confidence and promised to do all he could to assist in bringing a successful conclusion to this case. The team shook hands with the Minister who again impressed on them how important it was for Spain to solve this case as quickly as possible and to bring the culprits to trial. He was then taken back to the airport for his return flight to Madrid.

By the end of the day, arrangements had been made for flights to Moscow via Paris commencing late tomorrow morning after their passports were due back from the Russian Consulate.

Martin returned to his hotel to pack his case for the trip. He told the hotel staff he would be checking out the next morning but may return in a few days depending on what eventuated in Moscow. He thanked them for helping to make his stay in Bilbao so enjoyable despite the turn of events that he had found himself involved with.

He called Isabella and invited her for dinner that evening apologising for the short notice and explaining that the investigation had suddenly taken an unexpected twist which meant that he would be flying to Moscow the next day. Her offer to take him along the coast the following weekend to see the cave paintings would have to wait for another opportunity.

When she arrived at the hotel an hour later, he was knocked over by how beautiful she was. She was wearing a smart business suit and her long dark hair was loose and flowed over her shoulders.

They sat in the bar and drank a vodka cocktail as a symbol of his continuing adventure now heading in the direction of Russia the next day.

The conversation was mainly about Melbourne and its reputation for being a cultural city. "It has been named *'Most Liveable City in the World'* a number of times and although it is now suffering a strain on its infrastructure due to a population explosion, I still feel it is a great place to live," Martin said.

"We are very fortunate, there are theatres and concert venues which are close to the Victorian Police Complex and my office in the Fraud Squad which is downtown a short tram ride away. I sometimes attend a play or a concert by the Melbourne Symphony Orchestra after work and if the weather is fine, I walk there from my office. The National Gallery of Victoria, where European, Asian and American art is displayed is in the same precinct so it is very handy for me and I visit often. Every year they stage a *'Blockbuster'* exhibition of paintings and sculpture loaned from prestigious galleries such as The Hermitage in St.Petersberg, The Tate in London and the Pompidou Museum in Paris.

These *'Blockbusters'* draw enormous crowds from all over Australia as well as tourists who happen to be visiting at that time. The NGV has a separate museum where Australian art is on show and this is located across the river on the edge of the CBD."

Around 9 o'clock they went into the restaurant and ate a marvellous meal during which she told Martin about her legal work and the types of cases she was involved in. He told her that his sister Barbara was also a lawyer and hoped that one day she would have the opportunity to meet her.

They then retired to his suite so he could show her the fantastic view of the Guggenheim Museum.

Settling down with drinks from the mini-bar, they discussed the murder investigation and the hunt for the stolen painting. Isabella told Martin that the people of Bilbao were extremely shocked at the enormity of this crime, and friends of hers had said that they found it hard to believe that such an event had occurred in this otherwise sleepy town.

What had started off as a friendly chat developed into a somewhat more intimate situation with both of them feeling very attracted to each other. Isabella was an extremely passionate lover and Martin was smitten by her beauty. This resulted in Isabella staying until the early hours of the morning. She then had to rush back home to get herself ready for a day in court.

Martin drifted off to sleep thinking about the wonderful evening they had spent together and how attracted he was to this beautiful and smart woman. Although he had only met Isabella a few days ago, it was like he had known her for quite some time. He had never felt like this with any of the women he'd had relationships with back in Melbourne. If this was what love was like, then he found it very much to his liking.

•••••••••••••••••••••••••••

CHAPTER 11

BILBAO - MOSCOW, OCTOBER 19

Despite only having a few hours' sleep after Isabella left, Martin was up early and checked out of the hotel. The desk clerk confirmed that his entire bill had been taken care of by the Federal Government in Madrid. A police car arrived to take him to the airport and Carlos, who was already in the car told him, "Our passports have been returned from the Russian Embassy and are waiting for us to collect at the Immigration office inside the airport."

The drive out of Bilbao was very pleasant along a winding road through a valley surrounded by rolling hills and Martin began to feel like he was on vacation again.

At the airport, their passage through immigration and customs was carried out smoothly thanks to instructions from the Government Minister.

The Air France flight departed on time and due to a tail wind, arrived at Charles de Gaul Airport slightly ahead of schedule.

They had an hour and a half wait for the onward passage to Moscow so they sat in a café and drank strong black coffee until their flight was called. Carlos told Martin that he had never been to Moscow before and was uncertain of the reception they would receive.

"The few Russians I have met previously were tourists who had contacted the police because they had been robbed whilst visiting Bilbao. The thefts had usually taken place in sleazy nightclubs where drugs and prostitution were the order of the day and there was little we could do to recover their lost items. They sometimes became hostile towards us blaming us for their stupidity and we have even had to escort some to the airport and put them on a plane to ensure they departed."

The flight was uneventful and on arrival at Moscow's Domodedovo Airport, they were cleared through Customs quickly due to an earlier telephone call from the police chief, Vladimir Sushkin. They were met by a driver holding up a placard with their names on. Martin was quite unused to such efficient and welcoming treatment. "I have been very impressed with the co-operation between the police, customs and immigration departments of these two different countries. I am now wondering if such co-operation existed within Australia between the different state and federal police departments. I would hope it operates as efficiently as I have experienced here."

They were whizzed through city streets that were busy with traffic and taken directly to police headquarters located at number 38 Petrovka Street in the Tverskoy District.

Martin couldn't help commenting on the number of Mercedes, Audis and BMW cars they saw on the way..... "Looks like it didn't matter that Germany lost World War II, they certainly appear to have won the war when it comes to selling luxury cars in a country that historically has been so anti-German!"

Martin was also amazed at the haphazard way cars were parked along the streets they drove along. Some were parked in spaces so small that although it was supposed to be parallel parking, the vehicle had been reversed into the kerb with the front of the car poking out onto the roadway. "Look at that" Martin exclaimed to Carlos, "there's one parked over a pedestrian crossing on the corner in front of the traffic light pole! Wouldn't get away with that in Melbourne but here in Moscow it seems that anything goes."

At police headquarters, they were taken immediately to Chief Inspector Sushkin's office and given cups of strong tea with small sweet cakes. As they already knew from their earlier telephone call, the chief inspector could speak some English but given a choice on home ground, preferred to have an interpreter on hand at the meeting.

Carlos did most of the talking mixing some Russian with German plus the odd bit of English and ran through the complete case history explaining Martin's involvement from the day of the murder.

Martin was a little suspicious of the friendly welcome and the hospitality having heard many times that Russians weren't usually co-operative with Western law enforcement representatives, especially in regard to art fraud. They had a chequered history with regards to this type of crime, particularly with paintings confiscated by the Nazis during the Second World War which later turned up in Russia.

Notwithstanding Martin's suspicions, the Chief Inspector appeared sympathetic to helping them but again explained, "You must understand that the suspect, Alexei Nagormy is extremely well connected. Permission would have to be sought from certain people in the Kremlin before you could make any approach to him or his business." He then suggested, "The best thing would be for you to check into a nearby hotel and spend a few hours sightseeing whilst I make a presentation to the relevant government officials. I must impress on them the nature of the alleged crime and the furthering of good relations between Russia and Spain."

A driver was provided to take them to a hotel just two blocks away from the police headquarters and after checking in, they were driven to Red Square where the driver escorted them to the spectacular multi-coloured onion domed St. Basil's Cathedral. After taking photographs of the exterior, Martin and Carlos wandered through the maze of separate little chapels that make up this incredible edifice.

It was a cool but sunny day and after their tour of the cathedral, they sat at an outdoor café in front of the Gum shopping complex. They invited the driver to sit with them and asked him to order coffee for them all whilst they asked him questions about the buildings surrounding Red Square. It turned out that the driver, Ivan, had spent some time in London working with Scotland Yard on a police exchange program that had been set up by President Mikhail Gorbachev when he broadened Russia's outlook under *'perestroika'*. He was able to converse in excellent English with a slight British accent.

He explained, "The huge building alongside where we are sitting was originally known as the *'Gum Department Store'* and was the exclusive shopping centre only accessed by the communist ruling elite during the Soviet era. The proletariat could only guess at the range of clothing, appliances and imported foods that were sold there and the party leaders in the Kremlin ensured that the doors were kept closed for all but the *'lucky few.'* These days, it is now open to everyone, providing they have plenty of money! All the well-known brand names are represented there and I am told that the shops here are as smart and stylish as those found in Paris or New York."

The driver continued after finishing his cup of strong black coffee, "The picturesque St.Basil's Cathedral was built in 1561 during the reign of Ivan IV and it is actually called the Cathedral of Vasily the Blessed. It is a major tourist attraction and is only occasionally used for church services."

After a pause, he continued, "The high red wall that runs the full length of Red Square along the opposite side to the Gum Department Store shields the buildings of The Kremlin from where the government rules this vast land. You can see from here a number of onion domed churches that are used mostly by government officials and their families."

After spending half an hour wandering through the Gum shopping complex without buying anything, Martin and Carlos agreed that the prices were beyond anything a regular police officer could afford.

When they emerged into the bright sunshine they decided to wander around Red Square for a while hoping they might see someone famous such as the President but all they saw were some bored uniformed soldiers standing guard around Lenin's Tomb!

A short time later, their driver received a call from headquarters instructing him to immediately take the visitors back to Inspector Sushkin's office. On arrival, the driver took them directly to his chief and Martin and Carlos thanked him for his help with their sightseeing. The Inspector smilingly told them, "I am pleased to inform you that permission has been granted for you to visit Alexei Nagormy tomorrow at his business address. I will arrange with my men to come to your hotel in the morning straight after breakfast and take you to his warehouse. You will be escorted there by a small squad of police from Moscow Police Headquarters. Those officers will have a search warrant giving them permission to look through the warehouse for the stolen painting."

They ate a traditional hearty meal of pork and dumplings in the hotel restaurant that evening. Whilst they were eating, Carlos suggested to Martin that this all seemed too easy after Inspector Sushkin's statement earlier regarding Alexei Nagormy's standing with the Moscow government. There was nothing more they could do now until they visited the warehouse tomorrow. Emails were sent to their respective offices advising of the latest arrangements.

They both retired early as the programs on Russian TV were dreadful. Typical of the shows Martin found when surfing through the channels was a re-run of a recent Eurovision Song Contest with the commentator obviously complaining that the voting was rigged as the Russian entrant had finished up with only a handful of votes.

CHAPTER 12

MOSCOW, OCTOBER 20

After a good night's sleep and a leisurely breakfast, Carlos and Martin were picked up around 10.00 in a large Russian built Lada police 4-wheel drive with two uniformed officers to escort them. They were driven to Alexei Nagormy's warehouse by the same policeman who had taken them to Red Square the day before. The warehouse was located in a run-down industrial area of Moscow. On the way there, Martin observed to Carlos, "Many buildings are in a very poor state of repair, particularly the Soviet era grey concrete high-rise apartment houses. Most of the balconies are so cracked and broken they look as though they would collapse if anyone dared to walk out onto them. The buildings appear to be in such decrepit condition, it is hard to believe anyone lives in them." Carlos asked their driver who had overheard Martin's comments, "Does anyone actually live in these derelict buildings?" and he replied, "Yes, as far as living conditions are concerned, particularly in Moscow, not much has changed in public housing since President Gorbachev's 'perestroika'. It was really tough living under communism but for some people it's even worse now." He paused to concentrate on his driving for a minute as the vehicle had become stuck in a traffic jam.

He went on, "These terrible buildings have only one kitchen and one bathroom on each floor that must be shared by all the residents on that floor. Even with these awful conditions, the apartments are generally completely full with families with little money. Because the rents are only a few roubles a month, there are long lists of people waiting to move in the moment any become vacant."

To hammer home the point, he finished up by saying, "I know about this from personal experience because my wife and I have been waiting for more than two years to get one of these places. With my paltry police salary, we haven't enough money to afford anything better!

On my days off, I have a job as a security guard at a bank to increase my income and fortunately the security agency pays me in cash as police employees are not supposed to take on second jobs. It is common knowledge that some police officers take bribes but this depends on the position they have in the force. Traffic cops are in a perfect situation for this. Whenever they stop a driver for an alleged offence such as speeding or going through a red light without stopping, they offer the chance not to have a ticket in exchange for a small fee. My work is mainly in the office assisting the chief and driving him around so does not bring me face to face with offenders very often so I am always looking for other means to supplement my income."

On arrival at the warehouse, they were greeted by a pleasant young woman who introduced herself as Olga Petrova and told them she was the personal assistant to the company's owner, Alexei Nagormy. She took them immediately into a meeting room where a large samovar was set up and cups of tea were offered to everyone.

The four policemen sat sipping tea and nibbling delicious little cakes and chocolates that were handed around on expensive looking antique dishes. After a half hour had passed and there had been no sight of the person they wanted to see, Martin remarked to Carlos, "I think it's time to inquire when Alexei Nagormy is likely to grace us with his presence."

The moment Carlos posed the question to the receptionist, she suddenly looked quite concerned and turned to the two Moscow policemen and spoke to them rapidly in Russian. Carlos told Martin that it was too fast for him to understand so he asked the English speaking police officer that had driven them here what was going on. He embarrassedly replied, "I regret to inform you that the person you wanted to meet apparently flew to Paris last night and is now on his way to South America on urgent business!"

Carlos then asked him to tell the woman that they didn't want to waste any more time sitting around waiting to see someone who had departed Russia and was now heading off to the other side of the world, They would immediately wish to have a look around the premises. At this point, one of the Moscow policemen brought out the warrant which she read and smilingly agreed that they would now be taken on a tour of the warehouse.

Martin and Carlos knew that if she readily agreed to show them around it would be a useless exercise. "Obviously, Alexei Nagormy's government contacts warned him of our pending visit and he skipped town in a flash… no doubt taking the stolen painting with him," Martin quietly remarked to Carlos.

"To satisfy the Chief Inspector back in Bilbao, we must carry out a thorough search anyway, so at least we can categorically confirm that the painting is not still here," Carlos replied.

The warehouse was full of valuable looking antiques including a large collection of what could have been ancient Persian and Afghan carpets and rugs. As Martin had no experience with this type of artisan work he was unable to say whether they were genuine or not. "My gut feeling is that this guy is a crook and therefore the carpets and rugs are probably imitations made in low labour cost countries such as India and Bangladesh."

After spending a couple of hours looking through the racks and shelves without seeing a two metre long plastic pipe or a three metre by two metre Jackson Pollock painting, they thanked the woman and returned to Moscow Police Headquarters to report the disappointing result of their search to the Chief Inspector.

Inspector Sushkin was visibly upset after his two officers reported what had occurred during their morning visit to the warehouse. Though he risked being subsequently hauled over the coals by his superiors, he told Carlos and Martin that he would immediately track the flights and destination of the elusive Alexei Nagormy.

"By the way", he said, "while you were out this morning, I was contacted by the local Interpol operatives and they told me that they had come up blank after making inquiries as to whether any Russian oligarchs were interested in buying the stolen painting." He went on, "They also said that they would continue to investigate and let me know if they hear anything, but frankly I doubt they will do any more since I told them that our suspect had just taken off to the other side of the world. They would probably advise their colleagues in South America to be on the lookout for a Russian trying to sell a large stolen painting but at this stage, the actual destination of Alexei Nagormy was not known."

As it was expected that checking into the destination of Alexei Nagormy would take a little time, Inspector Sushkin suggested that the visitors make use of their short visit to Moscow by taking a walk to nearby cafes and shops. He asked them to return in a couple of hours.

The two men then strolled down the street and after poking around a number of souvenir shops, they both settled on buying similar gifts to take home for their families - sets of Matrioska Dolls! Martin wanted a set to give his mother and Carlos bought a set for his 8 year old daughter.

Later, they stopped at an outdoor café and drank strong cups of coffee whilst they discussed the latest turn of events.

As this café had free Wi Fi, Carlos and Martin sent emails to their respective superiors to update them of the situation.

On returning to police headquarters, Inspector Sushkin told them, "We have established that Alexei Nagormy is on his way to Brazil and that he has reserved a suite at the Sofitel Hotel on Copacabana Beach in Rio de Janeiro. He will be arriving there this evening on an Air France direct flight." He then handed them a photograph of Alexei Nagormy to enable them to recognize him if and when they caught up with him. This was another bit of helpful information provided by the Moscow Police Chief that could get him into hot water with the State authorities if they ever found out. Carlos and Martin thanked him for his hospitality and assistance and went back to their hotel to call Bilbao to report the latest news.

After Carlos had told his boss of Alexei's latest movements, Chief Inspector Segueros told them to sit tight and he would get back to them within an hour. In fact, he called back after only 20 minutes and told them that they were arranging flights for them to go to Rio di Janeiro the next day. Because Australians are required to have a visitor's visa, Martin would have to take his passport to the Brazilian Embassy in Moscow this afternoon to obtain a visa. A special permit was being rushed through as Brazilian visas normally take quite some weeks to obtain.

"Fortunately, I don't need a visa as Brazil and Spain have a mutual agreement to allow their citizens to travel freely between our two countries," Carlos told Martin.

The Chief Inspector also told them that the murder suspect had not been formally charged but was being held in custody pending further inquiries. They would have to charge him soon as they are unable to hold him indefinitely unless they applied for and were granted a special court permit which would have to be instigated by the State Prosecutor.

The delay in charging the killer was because they needed Martin to be on hand as he was the prime witness and it was hoped that he would be returning to Bilbao very soon.

They took a taxi to the Brazilian Embassy in Moscow and because he is an Australian, Martin was required to fill in a lengthy application form for a visitor's visa. The Spanish government had made arrangements via their embassy in Moscow to pay the visa fees earlier in the day when the rushed arrangements had been made with the Brazilian Embassy in Madrid. It took most of what remained of the day to complete the formalities but eventually, Martin's passport was stamped and they returned to their hotel.

Back at the hotel, they found a message from Bilbao detailing their flight arrangements for the following day.

That evening they went to a nearby nightclub which was somewhat more appealing than sitting watching the old Eurovision re-runs on TV in their hotel rooms! There was a floor show with very attractive topless dancers and the vodka was flowing freely amongst the mostly male customers. Carlos and Martin decided to keep their heads clear so they could face the early departure the next morning in good shape.

On the way back to the hotel, Martin remarked to Carlos that he was disappointed with Interpol's efforts. "Despite having spoken with my contact at Interpol prior to our departure to Moscow, they hadn't made any attempt to contact either myself or you whilst we were in Moscow. They had only made a brief contact with Chief Inspector Sushkin saying nothing of any real consequence."

"I suspect that Interpol's work within Russia may be somewhat hampered by corrupt officials and their local operatives are reluctant to stir up trouble or they could find themselves imprisoned over trivial matters," Carlos replied.

Martin asked Carlos to tell him about his family. "I met my wife Sandra, at high school and we dated right up until we graduated. She went on to study accountancy and I headed for the Police Academy as I had wanted to join the force from an early age. Not long into my training I decided I wanted to be a detective. Around this time, we married and honeymooned in the Canary Islands. Afterwards, we bought a tiny apartment in Bilbao and Sandra started a small accounting business run from a home office. A year later, our daughter Julietta was born and she is now at kindergarten. Sandra's accounting business has grown so much that she now employs two people and is about to move into a small office in town. With my detective's salary and her income from the business we are now looking around to buy a house with a garden for Julietta to play in. We have a happy marriage and are enjoying life to the full."

Carlos then asked Martin if he was married or had a steady woman friend. "I've actually had one serious relationship that I thought would lead to marriage but she broke it off saying she couldn't go through life worrying every night if her policeman husband was going to return home," he replied, "But right now I am as free as a bird and involving myself in my work and hoping to advance further up the chain of command in the Victorian Police Force." He decided not to tell Carlos of his recent evening with Isabella because she was such a close relative of the Chief Inspector.

They soon retired to their hotel rooms as the following morning required an early start for a long day of travelling to the other side of the Atlantic Ocean.

....

CHAPTER 13

MOSCOW TO RIO DE JANEIRO OCTOBER 21

Carlos and Martin had to be up and out of the hotel before dawn as their departure from Moscow airport to Paris had to get them there in time to change planes for a direct flight to Rio de Janeiro. They only had an hour to get from one side of the massive Charles de Gaul airport to where the Air France flight AF444 was leaving for Rio at 9.20am and in fact they found themselves having to run not to miss the plane.

Once comfortably settled on the aircraft, they sat back and enjoyed some great French cuisine during the almost 12 hour flight across the Atlantic Ocean.

They discussed strategy during the flight and decided that the best plan would be to follow Alexei whenever he went out of the hotel and to do this they would have to ask for help from the local police.

On arrival in Rio de Janeiro, they were surprised to see a uniformed officer holding up a sign with Carlos' name in large letters. It appeared that Chief Inspector Segueras was a step ahead of them all the way! The officer initially started speaking Portuguese but soon changed to English when Carlos explained that Martin was Australian. He drove them to the Sofitel Hotel overlooking the beautiful Copacabana Beach where they were met by an inspector from the Rio fraud squad.

He introduced himself as Inspector Manuel Filibi and said that he was the senior investigating officer with the Brazil National Police based in the Rio de Janeiro division. As it was well into the evening by this time, they would all dine together in the hotel restaurant once Carlos and Martin had checked in and freshened up. They agreed to meet at 9.00 to plan the next move in the hunt for the elusive painting and the criminal behind the theft.

Later in the dining room, over a glass of Argentinian Malbec, Carlos described in detail the events that had led them to Rio de Janeiro and how important it was to catch the Russian with the stolen painting in his possession. "Unless we apprehend him with the painting, we would not be able to make the charges of theft and murder hold up in court."

Inspector Filibi who was not in a uniform, told them, "The Rio police have confirmed that he was booked in at this hotel but have not seen him as yet. We are currently arranging to have 24 hour surveillance on the hotel and the moment he is seen to be leaving the hotel, he is to be followed and his ultimate destination reported back to our team. We assume that this Alexei fellow won't be carrying such a huge painting on his initial visits to meet and negotiate with potential clients. I have instructed my men that no approaches are to be made until such time as he was actually seen in possession of the large tube he is carrying the painting in. It is also assumed that he has deposited the painting in a self-storage warehouse somewhere between the airport and Copacabana on his arrival in Rio de Janeiro so it could be anywhere in this sprawling metropolis."

Carlos provided Inspector Filibi with a photo of Alexei Nagormy and the inspector then arranged for the surveillance team to be installed at the hotel. After contact details were exchanged, it was approaching midnight and Carlos and Martin found their eyelids drooping. They bade the inspector goodnight and headed off to their respective suites for some much needed sleep. Before switching off his laptop and crawling into bed, Martin called Isabella on Skype and had a quick chat to let her know he was now in Brazil. She hadn't spoken to her uncle for a couple of days so was unaware that the pursuit had now taken him to the other side of the world after his trip to Russia.

He was pleased to hear that the case she had been working on had finished and she had achieved a successful outcome for her client.

....

CHAPTER 14

RIO DE JANEIRO, OCTOBER 22

Fortunately, they weren't disturbed during the night and managed to catch up on some of their lost sleep. This resulted in them getting up later than had been the case with their early starts recently. They met in the dining room around 9.00 for a sumptuous buffet breakfast that was so extensive, Martin didn't know where to start.

He was more accustomed to country motels in rural Australia where the normal fare was bacon and eggs on toast so was not used to the gourmet offerings in 5 star hotels such as this. He decided he could very easily learn to enjoy this kind of luxury, especially when someone else insists on paying the bills!

They were just starting their second cup of coffee when Carlos' mobile phone rang. It was one of the surveillance police telling him that they had followed Alexei Nagormy out of the hotel early that morning and he had taken a taxi to a very large jewellery store along the beachfront at Ipanema. He had now been inside the jewellery store for more than an hour and a half and they were watching for him to come out again. The officer wanted to know if he was to enter the shop and look around and Carlos asked him to remain outside as they did not want the Russian to become suspicious and realise that he was under surveillance.

Despite the policeman being in plain clothes, some people could spot a cop a mile away and Alexei Nagormy would certainly be the kind of person who would always be on the lookout to check if he was being followed.

Carlos called Inspector Filibi and asked about the owner of the jewellery store and was told that this was one of the largest companies of its kind in all of South America with branches in most capital cities and major airports. "The de Gomez family, who own this company, are reputed to be art collectors on a grand scale so it is not surprising that Alexei Nagormy might have chosen them as a potential customer for the stolen painting." He continued, "The family lives in a huge mansion completely walled off from the prying eyes of the public and could easily have a painting hanging in the house that the people outside wouldn't know about or ever have an opportunity of seeing. On the other hand, the de Gomez family are renowned for being extremely honest in their business dealings so I would be very surprised if they would consider buying an art work that didn't have a legitimate provenance."

Inspector Filibi then told Carlos… "I have decided that once the Russian has left the store, I will go there myself and question the owner as I feel this is a delicate situation requiring discretion and one that should be carried out at a high level. I do not want to upset this family as they are on speaking terms with the Brazilian President as well as other top officials including my boss, the Commander-in-Chief of this region!"

The morning dragged on after the phone call and Carlos and Martin decided to take a walk along the tiled promenade that stretches for kilometres along Copacabana Beach. They saw the part of the beach where the volley ball matches were played during the 2016 Olympics. It still had nets and courts marked out and obviously this area is always used for that sport. It was a warm sunny morning and plenty of people were on the beach enjoying the springtime sunshine. There were even a number of hopefuls surfing already although the waves were not particularly high.

Around 11.00, the surveillance officer called to say Alexei Nagormy had left the jewellery store and hailed a taxi. Carlos and Martin immediately turned around and walked back to a spot opposite the entrance to the hotel to wait and watch if he returned or had headed off somewhere else. If the latter, the police trailing him would call in with a new location.

Whilst they were waiting, Martin pointed out to Carlos that drivers in Rio parked their cars in such small spaces that they were actually touching bumpers! There was a row of cars opposite and every one was touching the next car front and back. They assumed that people left their cars parked in neutral and without the parking brake on so others can push the car in front forward to get their own car out when they returned. Most of the cars were small Renaults and Peugeots so it was even possible they were lifted and moved in sideways suggested Carlos.

This was the second time Martin had pointed out strange parking habits to Carlos, first in Moscow and now in Rio de Janeiro. Carlos responded… "I have been to Paris a number of times and French drivers park their cars just like the Rio drivers with bumpers touching. That beautiful city is so jammed up with motor vehicles that it is the only way Parisians can fit their cars into the tiny spaces that are left along the streets. Fortunately Bilbao is not an overcrowded city so we don't have this problem."

Ten minutes later, a taxi pulled into the hotel entrance and the person they recognised as Alexei Nagormy hopped out, paid the driver and entered the hotel. They sat at a kiosk with a clear view of the hotel entrance and waited patiently but by early afternoon he had not re-appeared. They went back into the hotel and sat in Carlos' suite whilst he emailed a report through to Bilbao.

There was a message from Chief Inspector Segueros telling them that the trial for the man accused of the murder on the funicular would be postponed until such time as Martin was available to give evidence. The email also mentioned that it would be good if they could wrap up the case quickly as the expenses were now mounting considerably. The Police Minister was being questioned in parliament about the time it was taking to catch the Russian mastermind and the burgeoning high costs in bringing this criminal to justice!

The officer in charge of the surveillance police called to say that there had been a shift change of personnel and two new plain clothes officers were now established outside the hotel, one at the main entrance and the other watching the doorway in the side-street.

Carlos and Martin went back outside and in the side-street found a small café where they could sit at a table on the footpath and have a view of the hotel side entrance.

Despite their training for keen observation skills, they were unable to spot the surveillance officer who was somewhere around there. This was definitely a good sign and meant he knew how to blend into the background!

About two o'clock, Carlos' phone rang. It was the policeman watching the front entrance who told him, "Alexei Nagormy has just left the hotel and driven off in a large white van carrying only his suitcase. I am about to follow the van and will keep you informed as to its destination."

They went back into the hotel and asked at the front desk if Mr. Alexei Nagormy had checked out and were told that he had. There was nothing they could do now but wait for further information from the surveillance police.

Martin was getting somewhat anxious now as Alexei appeared to be leaving Rio in a hurry and could be heading who-knows-where else in this vast country or even further afield. He told Carlos, "It is likely that Senor de Gomez was in fact the person who had posted an inquiry on the internet looking to purchase a large modern painting and has turned down the offer from Alexei Nagormy because of its lack of provenance."

Martin tried to work out in his mind what Alexei would do now that the potential client here had not wanted the painting. All he could come up with was that it was possible that Alexei Nagormy had a list of other potential art collectors in this part of the world and would keep going until he succeeded in making a sale.

There was another possibility that Martin suddenly thought of and he spoke aloud even though he was alone at the moment....... *'What if all this running around was a smokescreen to put us off the track and all along Alexei had a real client somewhere else in the world just waiting for him to arrive with the kind of painting he had ordered?'*

There was a very real chance that the expense of tracking him down would prove too much for the Spanish authorities and they would call off the chase. He was looking out of the hotel window deep in thought and noticed that the traffic was logjammed as it was approaching the afternoon peak. This was obviously going to make it difficult for the surveillance police to keep up with Alexei.

He went to Carlos' suite and knocked on the door. Carlos opened up and was holding his phone to his ear. His expression was one of annoyance and Martin wondered what the latest bad news was. A few minutes later, Carlos disconnected from the call and told Martin, "The Rio police had shadowed the van right across the city in extremely heavy traffic to somewhere near the huge stadium where the 2016 Olympic Games had been held. Just as they were getting close enough to carry out a stop-and-search operation, a truck came out of a side street without stopping and smashed into the police car. In only a few minutes, the roads in the area were blocked with cars and trucks, some of which had piled into the ones in front. According to the officer who reported the bad news, it was a chaotic scene with the whole area now looking like a war zone. By the time they cleared the mess and another police car arrived to help them, they had well and truly lost sight of the white van. They radioed for assistance from the police air wing and a helicopter was deployed to help in the search. The van's registration number has been sent to all police cars currently patrolling the Rio streets and all we can do now is once again sit and wait."

By evening, Carlos and Martin were feeling very dejected and when they finally received a call from the Rio Police Chief, their morale dropped even lower. It seems that the fugitive had once again flown the coop….. The van was found abandoned at the international airport and Alexei had boarded the last flight for the night to Santiago in Chile. "Yes", replied the Chief when questioned about the long white tube, "it had been checked in as excess baggage." Carlos looked at Martin and grimaced.

Inspector Filibi went on, "I had immediately contacted my counterpart at police headquarters in Santiago and requested assistance in arresting the Russian when his flight arrived. Decades of mistrust and occasional conflicts between some of the South American countries has resulted in a distinct lack of co-operation between our police forces. It is my hope that in this day and age, things might have improved significantly so that we will receive reasonable co-operation from our neighbours in Chile. Unfortunately, this proved not to be the case in this instance. Whilst waiting to find out if they would help, we checked with the airline and they confirmed that the flight had landed and all the passengers had collected their luggage. Because of Chilean officialdom and government red tape, it had taken some hours to get a positive response from the Santiago police. By that time, Alexei Nagormy had long since departed from the airport with his package."

Carlos emailed the Chief back in Bilbao requesting instructions whether to follow or not. Meanwhile, Inspector Manuel Filibi invited them to dine with him at his favourite eating place, a marvellous Brazilian barbecue themed restaurant set in a park overlooking a lake.

This is a place particularly suited for carnivores as a seemingly endless supply of barbequed meat is brought to the table on long skewers and served in huge quantities. The waiters continue bringing the meat as long as the diner keeps a small round disc face up on the table that says 'YES'. When customers have had enough, they turn the disc over to read 'NO' and the waiters walk past without stopping!

Over dinner they discussed their disappointment at being so close to the man behind the murder and theft of the valuable painting. They agreed that unless they had actually been able to apprehend Alexei Nagormy with the painting in his possession, an arrest would have been fruitless, particularly with his highly placed connections in Moscow.

Inspector Filibi told them about his meeting with the jewellery store owner who confirmed that Alexei had shown him a photograph of a very large abstract painting that was for discrete sale.

"When Señor de Gomez asked if Alexei Nagormy had the appropriate provenance for this painting, he had replied that there was some sort of technical issue holding up the document but this should be resolved shortly. Señor de Gomez was not told who the artist was but was assured that it was a person of very high esteem and the chance to acquire one of his paintings was a very rare opportunity indeed."

The inspector had then showed Señor de Gomez a photo of the stolen Jackson Pollock painting and he nodded his head saying that was the same painting that had been offered by the Russian dealer.

Because Señor de Gomez would not consider buying a painting without a provenance at this time, they did not discuss price. As he is an avid art collector, he suggested to Alexei Nagormy that he might be interested if he could return another day with the relevant documents proving ownership of this painting. Alexei Nagormy had then departed in a somewhat angry mood mumbling and grumbling unintelligible words in Russian as he hurried out of the store.

The inspector then told them, "We have been able to track some of the movements of the Russian after the police car was involved in the accident. I had ordered some of the patrol cars that were added to the chase to look out for a self-storage warehouse along the main road on which the van had been travelling along.

In fact there were only two such places between the city and the airport and on making inquiries at both, our men struck it lucky with the manager at one of these places. He had watched a large white van enter and the driver had then asked one of the warehousemen if he would help load a long white tube into the vehicle before hurriedly departing within a few minutes. The small storage locker had only been rented two days before and a full month's rent had been paid in advance in cash."

While they were relaxing after gorging themselves with skewer after skewer of delicious beef, lamb and chicken, cooked to perfection and before tackling the array of desserts laid out on a long self-serve table, a text message came through from Bilbao instructing them to continue the pursuit of the Russian.

Inspector Filibi offered to assist with making their airline reservations for the flight to Santiago and if possible, introduce them to any contacts he might have with his Chilean colleagues. He optimistically went on to say, "Hopefully they may be more inclined to assist in this investigation as it originated in Spain and not Brazil. Meanwhile, Interpol have been advised of the latest developments and the current whereabouts of Alexei Nagormy and the painting."

Interpol told Inspector Filibi that they had since established that Alexei Nagormy had a diplomatic courier stamp in his passport which meant that he didn't have to obtain short-term visitor's visas before entering most countries. This was particularly convenient for someone who decides to go from country to country at a minute's notice.

They were driven back to their hotel where they made arrangements to check out the next morning. Martin emailed the Victorian Police Commissioner back in Melbourne with the latest news as well as letting his mother and sister know where he was now, and would be tomorrow, before shutting down the laptop for the night.

As he nodded off, he imagined himself taking part in a 21st Century adaptation of *'Around the World in 80 Days!'*

....

CHAPTER 15

RIO DE JANEIRO – SANTIAGO   OCTOBER 23 & 24

Martin and Carlos were taken to the Rio de Janeiro airport immediately after breakfast and followed a slow-moving line of people through Immigration, Customs and security checks. They finally boarded the LATAM Airlines flight which departed for Santiago mid-morning. The flight lasted almost 5 hours and as they approached the Chilean border, Martin had his first sight of the magnificent Andes mountain range.

He was overawed by the spectacle and glad he had chosen the window seat for this flight.

On arrival, they quickly passed through Customs and Immigration (no visas required for Chile) and were met once again by a police officer holding up a placard with their names on. The Chilean police superintendent had been contacted the night before by both Inspector Filibi from Rio de Janeiro and Chief Inspector Segueras from Bilbao, so was well aware of the importance of the mission the two detectives were on. "In my limited experience dealing with South American countries, I would guess that the Chilean police would be much more accommodating and helpful to another Spanish speaking force such as ours in Bilbao than the Portuguese speaking Rio de Janeiro police," Carlos suggested to Martin.

They found Santiago airport to be somewhat rundown and in need of renovation and they were glad to get outside and into the sunshine.

Carlos was feeling quite at home now that he was able to converse with the driver in his native tongue again. He translated for Martin, "I learnt that Alexei Nagormy had been tracked to a 5 star hotel situated high on a cliff overlooking the Pacific Ocean. He had arrived the night before and since they set up surveillance this morning, had not left the hotel. They guessed he would be making telephone calls to arrange appointments with prospective art lovers."

It was suggested that Carlos and Martin stay at a different hotel close by just in case Alexei Nagormy may have been given descriptions of them by the Russian authorities after their short stay in Moscow. He might also have seen them hanging around the hotel in Rio de Janeiro.

Alexei Nagormy was staying at the Miraflores Park Hotel and they were to be taken to the Marriott Hotel which was a block away also overlooking the ocean. On the way to the hotel, they stopped at the Santiago police headquarters and met with the Chief Inspector, Señor Hernando Mendez. They gave the Chief Inspector a rundown on events so far and he said that he would provide whatever assistance they needed including two uniformed men and a car to take them wherever they needed to go whilst in Santiago.

Señor Mendez then addressed them, "I apologize for the messing around last night which enabled the Russian to pass through the airport before we were given approval to become involved. It was only after our Commissioner had spoken to your Chief Inspector Segueras in Bilbao that I was instructed to help in any way I could."

There were two undercover men stationed outside the Miraflores Park Hotel who would keep them informed of any movements from the hotel by the Russian. It was agreed that should the suspect be cornered with the stolen painting, the Chilean police would arrest him on a charge of being in possession of stolen goods. "We can legally hold him for up to 48 hours pending an application from the Spanish government to extradite him to Spain and personally, it would give me a lot of pleasure as I hold no love for Russians."

The weather was glorious and the view of the Pacific Ocean from their hotel was superb. Martin decided that if he partly closed his eyes and stared out to sea, he could just make out the eastern coastline of Australia some 11,500 kilometres away!

Despite the 'thrill of the chase' through countries he had only ever learned about in geography class at school, Martin was by now feeling somewhat homesick and looking forward to returning to Melbourne and his work there. Living out of suitcase for weeks now was starting to wear thin. Because he had only packed for a maximum of 2 weeks, he was finding that he had to wash shirts and underwear every two or three days instead of once a week when he was at home. Fortunately he had brought shirts that did not need ironing if he hung them on hangers in the shower to dry.

They were eating lunch when Carlos received a call from the surveillance team that the Russian had departed his hotel and was being driven in a private hire car to a destination south of Santiago. The Chilean police were tailing him and would keep Carlos informed if and when he reached his destination. They also said that he wasn't carrying any packages with him so they assumed the painting must again be hidden away somewhere between the airport and the hotel.

A couple of hours later, one of the police officers called to say they had followed him to a large modern winery, called *'Casillero Del Andes'* with a large sign at the entrance proclaiming, *'Makers of Chile's Finest Wines'*. Here he had met with senior management for a little more than an hour and then departed the winery as quickly as possible. He was observed looking somewhat angry as he stepped into the car and instructed the driver to head back to Santiago!

Martin and Carlos decided to walk along the cliff top until they found a spot where they could plainly see the entrance to the Miraflores Park Hotel. They positioned themselves behind a row of palms so that anyone looking in their direction from a couple of hundred metres away would not notice their prying eyes.

The police who had followed the suspect to the winery, called to say that after Alexei Nagormy had left, they questioned the vineyard manager and he told them that he had been shown a photograph of a very large modern painting which was for sale. The officer explained, `"The manager had agreed it would look great on an extensive bare wall in the reception area of the private accommodation section of the estate. Unfortunately, although he was impressed by the painting, and it would fit nicely on one of his walls; the price was way above anything he was in a position to pay."

The officer continued, "We then asked the manager how the visitor came to choose him as a potential buyer and he replied that the *'Casillero Del Andes'* website had a permanent inquiry page on the internet requesting offers from art dealers for paintings to adorn the walls of the estate. They had bought a number of paintings this way over the years but most were of relatively low value. The most expensive had been a large painting by one of Chile's better known modern artists, Josefina Guilisasti that was now hanging above the grand fire place in their public dining room. They had purchased it for $130,000 two years ago."

He told the police that the Russian had emailed him a few days ago to say he could be visiting Chile and if so, he would like to come to the winery to discuss a magnificent painting he was selling on behalf of a client. The painting being offered could be bought for five million dollars but the Russian said he was willing to negotiate on price if the winery was seriously interested.

He became suspicious when the dealer, Alexei Nagormy told him that this painting could not be hung in a public area at the winery at the moment because there were some people looking for it who claimed they had the moral rights to its ownership. Alexei Nagormy had told the manager, "It would be *'better for everyone'* if the painting was hung in the owner's private dwelling and its location was not publicised."

The two Chilean police officers were now on their way back to Santiago and would personally report in detail to Carlos and Martin at their hotel after they returned. The winery was located 150kms southeast from Santiago and Carlos estimated it would take at least two hours before the two policemen arrived back at their hotel. Whilst they waited, they decided to go to the Marriott and have some refreshments and discuss their next move. They still could not approach Alexei Nagormy without first knowing where the stolen painting was hidden, and they would have to tread carefully not to tip him off that he was being shadowed. The fugitive had already shown he was a master at staying a step ahead of his pursuers.

Just before 6.00 pm, Martin and Carlos and the two policemen sat on a bench watching the sun set over the Pacific Ocean discussing in detail what they had learnt from their visit to the winery. Following the second rejection from the list of people Alexei Nagormy thought were potential customers, Carlos felt that he may now decide that his target needed to be someone in the *'Billion Dollar Club.'* They felt that this narrowed the field somewhat to countries including the USA, Britain, China, Russia, India and Australia. Although now relatively close to the United States, Martin felt that Americans were unlikely to want to deal with a Russian and Alexei Nagormy would know this. Britain was also unlikely due to the long distance from his current location in South America.

While they were contemplating this, a taxi arrived at the Miraflores Park Hotel and Alexei Nagormy was seen getting out and hurrying into the hotel.

They sat observing the entrance for the next hour and a half but he did not reappear.

They decided to check the rear of the hotel to see if he could have departed this way but there was a security guard on duty there and he told them that only tradesmen and delivery people had come and gone through this door in the past two hours.

Carlos called Inspector Mendez and was informed that Alexei Nagormy had checked out of the hotel and it appeared that he must have left via the rear door posing as a courier. Carlos then requested that he have his men stop Alexei Nagormy's vehicle if seen to be heading for the airport. It was suggested that his vehicle be searched, and he had the plastic tube with the painting inside, he could be charged with theft of a major art work from the Spanish city of Bilbao. If such a situation arose, then Carlos and Martin would like to interview him at police headquarters.

Some time later, Inspector Mendez called back and told them, "My men had indeed caught up with Alexei Nagormy along the road approaching Santiago International Airport and he *was* in possession of a long white plastic tube. When the officers insisted on seeing what was in the tube, he smilingly took the cap off the end and invited my men to remove what was rolled up inside. What they found was not a painting but a very old decrepit looking Persian rug! He had a customs declaration describing the rug and had not broken any Chilean laws so they were unable to arrest or hold him." Once again the wily Russian had outsmarted them.

Chief Inspector Mendez went on to tell Carlos, "My men will continue to follow him to the airport and call in once they have established his destination."

There was nothing more they could do now but return to the hotel and wait for further news.

Around 11.00pm, Carlos received a call from Chief Inspector Mendez, "Alexei Nagormy has just boarded a LATAM Airlines flight to Sydney, Australia via Auckland, New Zealand.

He did not check any excess baggage so the whereabouts of the painting remains unknown at this time."

He continued, "I asked my office to check all other airline flights that you could take to follow Alexei Nagormy to Sydney and the best option would be to fly with the Australian airline Qantas. It has a non-stop flight from Santiago direct to Sydney departing at 2.30 pm tomorrow afternoon. This will have you arrive some fourteen hours later than the Russian but considerably earlier than the next LATAM flight."

Both Carlos and Martin immediately emailed their respective superiors with this latest dramatic turn of events and requested urgent responses whether to continue with this investigation or return to their respective bases. Obviously this latest destination of the fugitive Russian will add considerable costs to the already large expense bill incurred to date.

Because of the time differences between Chile, Spain and Australia, there was no way Carlos would get a reply until the next morning as Bilbao residents would not be up and around for some hours yet. On the other hand, there was a good chance that Martin would receive an immediate response because Australians were already at work by this time of the day there.

In any case they would have to wait till later in the day for the Qantas flight to Sydney which would depart during the afternoon. This would allow them to at least stay most of the morning at the hotel and correspond in detail with their respective offices before checking out. Meanwhile, Martin was determined not to let the Russian get away with this heinous crime so he made a decision to reserve two seats on the Qantas flight and then told Carlos they would sort out who pays later! When he called the Qantas booking office, they told him that fortunately the flight was not full and there was no problem allocating two seats for them at this late stage.

He quoted his credit card details and was told that their tickets would be waiting for them at the Qantas check-in counter at Santiago Airport. They would just have to show their passports for identification.

They called Chief Inspector Mendez and thanked him for his assistance. He responded, "I am sending a car tomorrow morning to bring you to police headquarters for a review of what transpired during your brief visit to Chile. I have to file a detailed report on our involvement in your case to my superiors.

This shouldn't take much time and afterwards, I will personally take you to the airport in plenty of time for your afternoon departure to Australia. I can get us into the LATAM Airlines Club Lounge until your flight is called and while we wait I would like to hear some things about both of your countries, neither of which I have ever visited."

The next morning they arose early so they could write their reports for their respective offices and then checked out of the Marriott Hotel. They were picked up by a uniformed officer and on driven to police headquarters. On the way, Martin and Carlos discussed the cunningness of Alexei Nagormy. He continued to stay a step ahead of them and they were almost admiring of the way he had somehow spirited the painting out from under their noses whilst substituting it for a rug somewhere along the way.

It was now apparent that the painting was on its way to Australia on a freight flight no doubt disguised as something else in order to get it through the Australian Customs. Australia has a reputation for being extremely suspicious of all packages entering the country although they are normally more interested in containerized shipments of goods, particularly those emanating from the Middle East or Asia. A package coming from South America would most likely be checked by sniffer dogs looking for drugs so this type of investigation would not present a problem for Alexei in this case.

Whilst they were with Chief Inspector Mendez, they received messages from Spain and Australia agreeing to Martin's decision which pleased both men and vindicated Martin for *'jumping the gun'*. They decided not to mention to their Chiefs that the flights to Sydney had already been reserved.

Martin emailed the Victorian Police Commissioner with their flight details and requesting assistance in getting Carlos through immigration on their arrival in Sydney and also to arrange with his counterpart at the NSW police headquarters to have someone meet them on arrival at the Kingsford Smith international terminal.

They were driven to the Santiago Airport and checked in for their Qantas flight. The smartly uniformed woman who attended to them and issued the boarding passes told them, "As the economy class section of this very large aeroplane is not fully booked, I had no trouble allocating seats for each of you on both sides of the aisle at an emergency exit which will give you more legroom." They thanked her for her assistance as this was something for which these two six foot plus policemen were very grateful.

Chief Inspector Mendez accompanied them to the LATAM Airlines Club Lounge and all he had to do was flash his official police badge and they were admitted immediately into this nicely furnished quiet haven away from the milling throng of the busy airport.

Helping themselves to a few of the delicious food items and drinks that were on offer at the buffet, they sat in a quiet corner of the lounge and told the inspector about some of the highlights of their respective countries. He was especially interested in hearing about Australia and Martin offered to show him around Melbourne should the inspector ever head *'Down Under'*. He replied, "I don't know anything about Melbourne, but ever since I saw a television documentary on Australia I have wanted to visit Sydney and attend a concert at the iconic Opera House. I am a lover of classical music and attend the Santiago Symphony Orchestra concerts whenever I have some hours free from my very busy work schedule." He told them about their beloved old concert hall, which in a typical Spanish way, has a name a mile long! It's called the *'Teatro Municipal de Santiago de Chile.'* It seems that opera, symphony concerts and plays are staged there continuously.

In what seemed no time at all, their flight was announced for boarding. Once again they thanked Inspector Mendez for his efforts and promised to keep him updated on the outcome of the case.

After they boarded the Qantas Boeing 777 for the more than 14 hour non-stop flight across the Pacific Ocean they found that they were in the same row but on opposite sides of the aisle with no-one beside them. This meant they could raise the armrests and stretch out across the seats when it came time to get some rest.

Once they were settled into their seats and the plane had taken off, Martin chatted on to Carlos about Australia. "I hope I'll get an opportunity to show you a few of the sights around Sydney. It's a beautiful city spread around a magnificent harbour with great surf beaches and lots of boating activities. Although I was born and raised in Melbourne, I know Sydney reasonably well having been there many times for work and have taken holidays there a few times. In my younger days I had a girlfriend who lived in Sydney and she tried unsuccessfully to teach me surfing."

They settled into the comfortable seats, watched a movie and a few hours later were served dinner. Both of them discussed how annoyed they were at the run-around Alexei Nagormy was giving them, but agreed that this made them more determined than ever to catch this guy and bring the chase to an end as soon as possible.

After watching another movie, they managed to relax a little before dropping off to sleep as the aeroplane hummed across the Pacific Ocean at 33,000 feet.

••••••••••••••••••••••••••••

CHAPTER 16

SANTIAGO TO SYDNEY OCTOBER 26

Martin and Carlos had managed to get some sleep between meals and watching first-run movies during the long flight, and were in reasonable condition when they arrived at Sydney Airport. Martin pointed out to Carlos that during the night they had crossed the International Date Line and had lost a day in doing so.

Because of the multi-national nature of the crime they were investigating, the Victorian Police Commissioner had requested the Australian Federal Police arrange for a representative to meet them at Sydney Airport. The AFP is based in the Capital, Canberra, and has jurisdiction in all states, similar in this respect to the American FBI.

This enabled both men to pass quickly through immigration and customs on arrival and they were taken to a special part of the airport where the AFP had offices.

The man in charge, Sergeant Barrie O'Donnell explained, "I received a detailed brief from Sir Charles MacPherson and we have been tracking the movements of the suspect since his arrival. We now have him under constant surveillance at his hotel. He is staying at the Four Seasons which is one of the most expensive hotels here. It is opposite Circular Quay, which is where the Sydney ferries ply backwards and forwards carrying commuters across our beautiful harbour and the huge cruise liners dock."

He went on, "From his hotel he would have a great view of our world famous bridge and opera house but I doubt that he would be very interested in looking at the scenery. Certainly, his mind will be concentrating on his financial situation with respect to selling the painting. From what we have learned so far, he would have run up a considerable amount of expenses and must now be anxious to recoup these as quickly as possible."

After checking his notes, Sergeant O'Donnell continued, "As the AFP had been supplied with a photo of Alexei Nagormy we had the Immigration Department officers carefully surveying every male passenger arriving on the LATAM Airlines flight from Santiago. This turned out to be very fortunate as he had entered the country using a forged Australian passport under the name of Ivan Gudonov. On checking government records, we found that there really had been a Russian of that name who had immigrated to Australia back in the 1960's but had actually passed away about a year ago. Because no-one yet knows where the stolen painting might be, the officers were instructed to allow him to enter without being questioned. We will keep him under surveillance until the painting has been recovered. If at any stage we feel he might be trying to flee the country for whatever reason, we can detain him and charge him with entering Australia on a forged passport. I can assure you, one way or the other you are going to get your man."

Martin then asked Sergeant O'Donnell if the AFP had learned anything else about Alexei Nagormy in the short time they have been involved in the case. "We have had discussions with some officials at the Spanish Embassy in Canberra who are keen to assist in any way they can. They told us that this guy is an extremely *'slippery eel'* and we intend to do our utmost to ensure he doesn't slip away under our watch."

He added, "On the question of the painting, the AFP had put out a search notice to all air freight forwarders and couriers to look for a two metre long tube with a bill of lading originating from either Chile or Brazil as it was unclear from which country it may have been dispatched.

We suggested that the contents are probably listed as an antique rug or a tapestry wall hanging. Unfortunately, there are hundreds of freight businesses moving thousands of goods into and out of Australia every day as well as moving them around the country so it is unlikely the AFP will find the carrier and its location quickly. Since the advent of internet buying, Australians have wholeheartedly embraced this form of shopping and the couriers and the postal service are inundated with packages. Despite the government continually increasing the number of customs personnel engaged in checking packages arriving into the country each year, they are having difficulty handling the number of goods arriving daily and some packages pass through with very little scrutiny."

The two globe-trotting police officers sat with Sergeant O'Donnell sipping coffee and recounted their adventures chasing Alexei Nagormy halfway around the world.

Thinking about what the sergeant had said a few minutes ago regarding not being certain which city the painting had been dispatched from, Martin put forward this scenario, "Alexei Nagormy may have left the painting in Rio de Janeiro with someone he knew, possibly another Russian businessman, until he found a buyer in Chile. He would then have it sent on to Santiago if the sale was successful. If not, he would have it dispatched from Rio de Janeiro to the next destination to meet him there. Meanwhile he had taken an old rug in a similar white plastic tube with him to Chile as a diversion. That is what he had with him when the Santiago police stopped him and searched what he was carrying as he was on his way to the airport. I am beginning to appreciate the sort of cunning this fellow operates under." Carlos nodded his head in agreement and said that he thought that Martin's suggestion was altogether believable.

No doubt the next move would depend on where the potential buyers might be located and they would have to be patient until the AFP surveillance team reported back on any movement from the Four Seasons hotel.

Australia has a small number of extremely well off families who could be interested in adding to their art collections although it was generally agreed that those who might look the other way when it came to buying a painting without the necessary provenance documents would be limited.

The AFP had started contacting some members of the families in the BRW *'Rich 200 List'* to tell them that they may be approached by a Russian art dealer who was currently in Australia looking for a buyer for a Jackson Pollock painting. The list of people contacted included billionaire families in Sydney, Melbourne, Perth and Brisbane whose fortunes had been made in businesses as diverse as shopping centres, clothing store chains, iron ore and coal mining as well as property developers in Western Australia and the Queensland Gold Coast.

Martin and Carlos were driven to an Ibis Apartment Hotel near Circular Quay to rest up and await further developments. Feeling extremely *'jet-lagged'* they both took a nap and then went for a walk so Martin could show Carlos the iconic Sydney Opera House. After Carlos had taken a number of photos including a *'selfie'* with the Opera House in the background they then continued walking through the nearby botanical gardens. From there they went to the Art Gallery of NSW where they spent a pleasant couple of hours.

Unfortunately, the gallery did not have a Jackson Pollock with which Carlos could familiarise himself.

They returned to their apartment where Carlos prepared a typical Spanish meal using some of the fresh vegetables and meat they had picked up at a nearby Woolworths supermarket. A home cooked meal was a welcome change from the airline and hotel food they had been eating since they left Bilbao almost a week earlier and Carlos proved that he was very competent in the kitchen. Whilst Carlos was busy in the kitchen, Martin telephoned his mother and sister to tell them that he was now in Sydney and there was a chance he would be home in a couple of days.

....

CHAPTER 17

SYDNEY OCTOBER 27

Martin and Carlos were picked up after breakfast and taken to the AFP offices in downtown Sydney where they were introduced to two men assigned to the case by Sergeant O'Donnell. Their names were Des Browning and Charles (Robbie) Robertson.

Des commenced their report, "The Russian had not made any telephone calls from his hotel room so we assumed if he was contacting potential buyers, he was doing this from public phones or had purchased a mobile phone with a pre-paid SIM card. These are readily available at convenience stores and supermarkets and make it very difficult for us to trace."

Robbie continued, "As of this morning, he has only been observed walking around the area near his hotel and had not ventured further than two blocks away. He had since returned to his hotel suite and the AFP continues to keep him under constant surveillance."

Sergeant O'Donnell joined the group at this point to inform them that the domestic airlines had been requested to contact the AFP if anyone by the name of Ivan Gudonov or Alexei

Nagormy made a reservation to fly out of Sydney but until now they had not been aware of any such inquiry or booking.

"A check with the freight and courier companies that morning resulted in no two metre long tubes being identified as having arrived in Sydney from South America." Sergeant O'Donnell then put forward a suggestion that it may have been consigned to a different city which made sense as Alexei Nagormy had proven to be smart in outfoxing the police from day one. He then instructed one of his assistants to get messages out to the freight and courier companies to check if any such item had been consigned to one of the other capital cities.

Around mid-morning, a call came through from the private secretary of a Mr. Joseph Rose, head of the family that controlled the Southern Cross shopping centres. They have malls throughout Australia and in a number of other countries including New Zealand, the USA and the UK. She explained to Sergeant O'Donnell, "Mr Rose received a call about an hour ago from someone speaking English with a heavy European accent requesting a meeting to discuss a large painting he has for sale. He gave his name as Ivan Gudonov.

As Mr. Rose had been contacted by the AFP yesterday and warned that this might happen, he had told the supposed art dealer that he might be interested and would get back to him after he had checked his appointment book for a suitable day and time." The caller had told him that he would phone back after midday as it may be difficult to contact him because he intended to do some sight-seeing around Sydney.

The secretary then asked, "Does the AFP want Mr. Rose to set up a meeting and if so, do you have some special procedures we are to follow?" Sergeant O'Donnell replied, "When Mr. Rose receives the next call from the Russian art dealer, he is to insist on seeing the actual painting as a photograph would not be enough for him to make a decision whether to purchase or not.

The meeting is to be set up at an address the AFP will provide as we do not want it to take place at either the head office of Mr. Rose's company or in a public place in case there are difficult consequences arising from any arrest." He went on, "Mr. Rose is to tell the Russian art dealer that the meeting will take place in a private house his company has for entertaining visiting guests, It is located in the North Sydney suburb of Wollstonecraft and the address will be advised once the two parties have agreed to meet." It would be an AFP *'safe house'* that is set in a large allotment with plenty of distance between the house and the prying eyes and ears of the neighbours on all sides. As things developed, these arrangements never had to be implemented because it turned out the meeting was not going to take place in Sydney after all!

Soon after lunch, the secretary called back. "Contact has again been made with the same person and he told us that if Mr. Rose insisted on the painting being presented at the meeting, it would have to take place in Canberra as that is where the painting was currently being stored. Mr. Rose then told him that this was most inconvenient as he did not have the time to head to Canberra at a minute's notice and he would have to reconsider his position."

The secretary went on to say that Alexei Nagormy then angrily told Mr. Rose that he would call back later that afternoon and if he didn't get a more positive response from him then he would offer the painting to another potential buyer.

Sergeant O'Donnell then asked the secretary to transfer the call to Mr. Rose because the arrangements for a meeting with the Russian in Canberra would require very careful planning and they needed to get together to work this out. A moment later Joseph Rose came on the line and invited them to meet in half an hour at his office which was in the centre of town.

Martin, Carlos, Sergeant O'Donnell and the two AFP assistants went down into the basement and were provided with a seven seater Toyota Land Cruiser to take them to the head office of Southern Cross Shopping Centres in Pitt Street, in the heart of the CBD. On arrival at the Southern Cross offices, they were directed by a security officer into an underground executive's car park and then escorted to the 26th floor where Mr. Rose's secretary greeted them as they came out of the elevator.

They were led into a magnificent boardroom and introduced to the Roses: the patriarch, Joseph, his two sons, Manny and Richard and a daughter, Raechel.

Whilst coffee and pastries were being served, Martin glanced at the collection of paintings hanging around the boardroom and was impressed by the variety and the mix of well-known Australian and European artists. He stood up and gave a brief outline of the theft from the warehouse of the West Coast Freight company in Bilbao and the subsequent murder on that city's funicular that he had happened to witness. He explained that this resulted in his being asked to assist in solving the case. Working with the police in Bilbao suddenly developed into a chase halfway around the world which had ultimately led them here to Sydney. They then got down to the business of how to set up the *'sting'* to ensure this slippery criminal did not escape the long arm of the law again.

Joseph had survived the Holocaust and had migrated to Australia in 1952 and over the decades had established a business that had become a world leader in shopping centre management.

According to him, his success was due to the wonderful country that had welcomed him from the horrors of the Second World War and he now considered himself an *'Aussie'* through and through. Because of this, he was willing to do whatever the AFP wanted him to do to catch the Russian crook. This would be his way of giving thanks to the country he now called home.

As the headquarters of the Australian Federal Police is based in Canberra, it meant that they had ample resources available if required, both in terms of personnel and equipment. This was a distinct advantage. The major stumbling block would be where the Russian wanted to hold the meeting as they were sure that he would not agree to any place proposed by the Roses.

Alexei Nagormy, alias Ivan Gudonov had proven to be a person who needed to be in command of the situation and therefore the venue would be one that best suited his plans.

They then discussed who would represent the family and Joseph Rose said that although he would ultimately take responsibility for whatever took place, he believed Manny would be the best choice as he was a very good negotiator. This was necessary as any offer made would have to appear to be genuine and there would probably have to be a cash deposit made before the painting would be presented for viewing.

Just then the secretary appeared at the doorway and told them that the Russian was on the phone and wanted to talk to Mr. Rose.

The call was to be put through to a conference telephone unit set in the centre of the boardroom table and Joseph told them that it automatically recorded the calls as they used it for meetings with their shopping centre managers around the world.

Alexei Nagormy started by saying, "I want to meet you at the Canberra Hyatt Hotel which I am informed is close to the Australian Parliament building at 3.00 o'clock tomorrow afternoon. I will be in the tea room and will have a small Russian flag standing in the sugar bowl in plain sight." Joseph Rose interrupted Alexei Nagormy at this point and said, "Mr. Gudonov, as I am not in the best of health to travel, I will be sending my son Manny to meet with you and he is empowered to negotiate a price on behalf of the family should he decide the painting would be a worthy addition to our extensive collection. Once Manny has spotted the flag, he will approach your table and introduce himself."

Before ending the call, Joseph Rose casually asked, "Will you be providing us with the provenance for the painting?" Alexei Nagormy replied, "The documentation has not yet been received here in Australia but should be available sometime soon. In the meantime, the painting should be kept locked away and not put on public display." Joseph Rose assured him, "This arrangement will be satisfactory, and assuming we like what you are offering enough to want to purchase it, I hope it won't be too long before we can bring the painting out of 'hiding' and show it to all our friends."

Joseph Rose told the gathering that he would have their company jet take them down to Canberra that evening and Carlos suggested that they stay in a hotel some distance away from where the Hyatt is located just in case that is where the Russian is staying.

Sergeant O'Donnell told the gathering, "I propose that you stay at the Rydges on Capital Hill which is not far from the AFP headquarters and is separated from the Hyatt Hotel by the area that not only has the magnificent Australian Parliament House, but most of the government offices. I know you are not here as tourists but as you are moving around it is worth noting that the public buildings located nearby are of wonderful architectural styles. They include the National Gallery, National Library and the High Court of Australia. These are all along the banks of the lake named after the American architect Walter Burley Griffin who designed and laid out the entire city of Canberra in the 1930's."

After thanking Joseph Rose for his co-operation, arrangements were made for Martin and Carlos to be taken to the Ibis Apartment Hotel to check out and collect their bags. They would then go with Sergeant O'Donnell to his home to pack his travel items and let his wife know that he would be away for a couple of days. After this, they would be driven to the Bankstown suburban airport just a short distance outside Sydney where many private aircraft such as the Rose's are kept. Manny would meet them there.

Despite the heavy afternoon traffic clogging up the roads around Sydney, they managed to get through it easily.... a little thing like flashing lights and a siren helps a lot when you're in a hurry!

By 7.00pm, they were on board a sleek Cessna Citation corporate jet and on the way to Canberra where they landed 45 minutes later.

An AFP car was waiting for them on arrival at Canberra airport and sped them to the Rydges hotel in 15 minutes. After checking in, they met in the bar for a drink before settling down for a pleasant dinner in the hotel dining room which is alongside an atrium filled with huge decorative pear trees.

During dinner they kicked around theories why Alexei Nagormy would have chosen Canberra for showing the painting and then Sergeant O'Donnell pointed out that being the Capital, all the foreign embassies were located here, including the Russian embassy of course! In fact, the embassies were in the area just behind the Hyatt Hotel.

"If I am right, the painting is most likely somewhere in the Russian embassy, and as long as it remains behind the embassy walls, we will not be able to get our hands on it." The more he thought about it, the more plausible it seemed. He went on, "This would also be why we have not been able to track the movement of the painting through normal channels such as the courier companies, because it would have been classified as a diplomatic package and not subject to customs examination. Alexei Nagormy's connection with the people at the top in Moscow has proven to be a most important asset for him and this has enabled him to continue being always one step ahead of his pursuers. It is unlikely he knows for certain that he is being followed here, but because the news of the theft of the Jackson Pollock painting has made headlines on TV and in newspapers around the world, he would be on the lookout for any signs that he was being observed by authorities." Looking at Carlos, Sergeant O'Donnell said, "I don't know if Martin has told you, but Jackson Pollock name is well known in Australia because of the controversy at the time it was purchased for the Australian National Gallery." Carlos nodded and replied, "Oh yes, Martin told me and my colleagues back in Bilbao all about it and I hope I have time while we are here to go the gallery and have a look at it."

After dinner, they all wandered to nearby Manuka, an upper class suburb with high end shops and many restaurants and bars. This is a popular place for Canberra's thousands of public servants to spend an evening unwinding from the difficult task of managing the country's affairs. It is always busy and has a wonderful atmosphere.

After a pleasant walk around the area, they returned to the hotel and settled down for the night.

CHAPTER 18

CANBERRA OCTOBER 28

Martin and Carlos were up and about early and had a leisurely breakfast in the hotel before meeting the others. Sergeant O'Donnell told them that he and his assistants were going in to their head office to put in their reports and make the necessary arrangements for covering the forthcoming meeting between Alexei Nagormy and Manny Rose. He would meet the visitors back at the Rydges Hotel for lunch around 1.00pm.

As they had the morning free to do other things, Martin suggested that he take Carlos to the National Gallery of Australia to show him the Jackson Pollock painting *'Blue Poles'* that he had expressed a desire to see the night before. Manny Rose told them that he had to visit people at the Southern Cross office in downtown Canberra during the morning, and would see them back at the hotel that evening after his meeting with Alexei Nagormy.

While they waited for the gallery to open at 10.00, he called the Police Commissioner in Melbourne to fill him in on what was happening and told him he believed they were finally getting close to wrapping up the case.

The National Gallery of Australia is a marvellous large modern building set alongside the lake that dominates the Canberra landscape. It contains some excellent works, having always had generous donations from private corporations, well-heeled individuals and of course, the Federal Government. This has enabled it to purchase many expensive artworks including the famous *'Blue Poles'*. The gallery security guard standing in that room told them that they were lucky to see it as it was shortly to be packed up and sent to England where it was going to be exhibited at The Tate Modern gallery in London for some months.

Martin was thrilled to be able to show Carlos the Jackson Pollock painting. "Despite it being the most looked at painting in the gallery, the consensus of opinion is that most Australians don't like it." He then explained to Carlos. "Some time ago, the gallery management believing it had been on display for far too long, decided to remove it from exhibition and store it in their extensive basement. There was such an outcry from the public, it was immediately returned to its usual place in the main gallery." Carlos studied it for some time and remarked, "I can't say that I understand what the artist is saying with all these squiggles and splotches of thick paint but I like it. Visually I find it very appealing." Martin then showed Carlos the large collection of paintings by some of Australia's favourite painters from the late 19th and early 20th centuries including

Tom Roberts, Arthur Streeton and Frederick McCubbin who depicted life in the colonies at the turn of the century.

He then led Carlos through the indigenous section of the gallery which is filled with hundreds of Aboriginal paintings, totems and a wonderful collection of hand woven baskets. Carlos had never seen anything like this before and wanted to spend more hours than they had available looking at them. Before they departed the National Gallery, Carlos told Martin, "Although I liked *'Blue Poles'*, those Aboriginal artworks were far more meaningful to me."

Martin had found Carlos a very caring and thoughtful individual since their first days together working on the case. They had grown even closer during their travels and this statement today caused Martin to really warm to him.

They returned to the hotel in time to meet up with the officers from the AFP for lunch. As they were settling into the meal, Sergeant O'Donnell told them of the arrangements now under way. "We have staked out the entire area around the Hyatt Hotel and have some men already seated inside the main dining room. Every entrance is under surveillance and cameras are in place all around the hotel." This case was being given the attention of a major international crime and Martin was staggered by the enormity of it all. Carlos told the gathering, "I have alerted the Spanish ambassador about what was going on here in Canberra today and they in turn were keeping the police in Bilbao as well as the Minister of Police in Madrid, informed of the latest situation.

Sergeant O'Donnell called Manny Rose on his mobile phone and told him that everything was in place for him to be at the Hyatt by 3.00pm to meet Alexei Nagormy. "Firstly, I must remind you that this fellow is going under the name of Ivan Gudonov so you must not call him by his real name or he will immediately know that he has been found out. We realise that due to its size, it is not possible for Alexei Nagormy to have the painting with him at this initial meeting. It's certain his first priority will be establishing the terms of sale and payment method. You are to go along with whatever he proposes and the AFP will be listening to the conversation through long range microphones that we have had installed in and around the public spaces at the hotel. Only the top management at the Hyatt are aware of our surveillance activities today. The staff has been told that we were installing equipment for a private function happening later this week."

Carlos, Martin and Sergeant O'Donnell were picked up around 2.30 and driven to the Hyatt Hotel where they were taken in via a rear entrance reserved for people who worked at the hotel. The AFP had taken over one of the guest rooms closest to the dining room.

The hotel is famous for its huge afternoon tea offering that has for many years been a popular Canberra daily event for well-heeled locals and a gathering place for the nearby foreign embassy officials. This would be the setting for the meeting between Manny Rose and the Russian.

The AFP surveillance room had three TV monitors in place and a special amplifier set up on a table with a number of earphones connected. The three men settled down to wait for the meeting to take place.

A couple of minutes after 3 o'clock, the CCTV camera over the front entrance picked up Alexei Nagormy entering carrying a large brief case. They watched him pass through the front door and then on the next monitor saw him walk along the hallway and into the dining room. The third camera was in the dining room and they observed him being seated at a table in the far corner of the room.

A few minutes later Manny Rose was seen entering the dining room and after a brief moment whilst he looked around the room, he spotted Alexei Nagormy sitting in the corner with a Russian flag poking out of the small vase on the table. Shortly after, the two men were in deep conversation and through their headphones the police could hear them reasonably clearly.

Following the introductions, the two men got down to business straight away. Alexei Nagormy described the painting in detail and then passed his I-Pad over to Manny Rose to show him a series of photos of this Jackson Pollock masterpiece.

Manny was struck by the bright colours in the painting and although it was difficult for most people to fully understand the meaning behind such an abstract work, he found it very attractive. He told Alexei, "I can easily see it hanging on one of the walls in my father's large house overlooking Sydney harbour or in the board room of the Southern Cross head office. Our family has a huge collection of art from all around the world but till now hasn't had a painting by Jackson Pollock."

He asked about the painting's provenance and received the same answer that the earlier potential buyers and his father had been told. "There are some difficulties that are currently being addressed by our lawyers back in Moscow and they are certain the problems will be resolved very soon. Meanwhile, the painting will have to be kept out of the public eye until the provenance becomes available." Manny Rose then asked, "What rights would a buyer such as my family have if the provenance documents did not come through?" Alexei Nagormy responded, "If such an unlikely event occurred, the money would be immediately refunded to the buyer on return of the painting." Manny Rose thought to himself that this would never happen...... they could say goodbye to their money.

The terms of sale were then proposed by Alexei Nagormy. "A one million U.S. dollar deposit is to be paid into a bank account in the Cayman Islands immediately, and once I have confirmation of the deposit, I will make the necessary arrangements to take you to see the painting. If after the viewing, you wished to proceed with the purchase, the balance of the money, nine million U.S. dollars is to be deposited into the same account. Once receipt has been acknowledged by the bank, the painting will be handed over." He went on to explain, "Due to the size of the painting, it is not framed and in fact is being transported rolled up inside a plastic pipe for protection from damage." Manny casually asked, "Where did you obtain this painting?" Alexei Nagormy obviously unaware of the publicity the theft had received in Australia immediately responded, "Our company purchased it from a South American art dealer who had run into financial difficulties. It is due to his company now being declared bankrupt that there is a delay in obtaining the provenance."

At this stage, the discussions were paused and afternoon tea ordered. This grand spectacle involved a series of carts being wheeled around the room with different delicacies on display that are then selected by the guests. Manny Rose had been here a number of times previously and knew the procedure so he explained to Alexei Nagormy how it all worked. Tea and coffee was then served to enjoy with the savouries, pastries and cakes.

Manny Rose excused himself to go to the bathroom and whilst there relieving himself, Sergeant O'Donnell came in and quietly nodded at him indicating he should go along with the proposal. He whispered, "The money to be outlaid would be backed by both the Spanish government and the insurance company that covered the Bilbao exhibition should anything go wrong."

Manny Rose then returned to the table and told the Russian, " *Mr. Gudonov*, I am now going to call my father to arrange for the immediate transfer of the million dollars from one of our offshore bank accounts to cover the deposit. As we have accounts in the USA, the transfer can be made very quickly electronically on an urgent basis, and even though it is night-time there, it does not require the American bank to actually be open."

Alexei handed over a small card with the Cayman Islands bank details and Manny Rose immediately called his father and passed on the instructions. He noted that the account was held not under a name but a *"customer identification number"* obviously to keep the account holders completely anonymous.

The two men then sat quietly enjoying the delicious afternoon tea as they waited for email confirmation to arrive on *'Ivan Gudonov's'* iPad that the deposit had been received at the bank.

They did not speak during this time but sat silently savouring the food and sipping coffee.

At 4.45, the message arrived that the money had been deposited into his account and *'Ivan Gudonov'* then told Manny Rose, "It will take a little time to arrange for you to see the painting as it was being stored inside the Russian Embassy. I will now make a quick call to the Embassy and tell them that I would like to bring a visitor there shortly to view the painting." As the Hyatt was very close to the embassy, they might as well wait around at the hotel until they were given permission to enter the embassy.

Meanwhile, to seal the deal, he ordered two glasses of the best Russian vodka the bar had on hand. After these were served, they sat quietly drinking while waiting for a message from the Embassy.

Back in the surveillance room where the police were watching these developments, Sergeant O'Donnell put through a call to his office and spoke to his superior about this turn of events. Turning to Martin and Carlos, he told them, "According to international law, we have no jurisdiction over what takes place inside a foreign embassy as it is classified as sovereign territory belonging to the country whose embassy it is. We can and will take possession of the painting once Manny Rose emerges with it but as long as Alexei Nagormy remains in the embassy we are not able to arrest him."

This was particularly worrying for Carlos as he wanted to nab him for the murder as well as return the painting to the museum. The assembled group acknowledged the clever tactic of Alexei Nagormy in using the Russian Embassy which gave him the best cover possible.

As the afternoon dragged on, refreshments were ordered to be brought to room 101 whilst they waited patiently for the next phase of the operation to commence.

Meanwhile, although it was early morning in Bilbao, Chief Inspector Segueras was in his office waiting anxiously for news from Australia. Meanwhile, he contacted his counterpart at the Paris headquarters of Interpol and asked him to see if there was any way they could freeze the Cayman Island bank account of a Russian criminal. Monsieur Pierre Dubois replied, "In general this type of bank has no interest in assisting police or foreign governments in such matters, particularly banks where very large accounts are held in order to avoid taxes in the customer's home country. There were recent revelations that many government officials including some prime ministers and presidents from around the world had billions of dollars hidden in accounts throughout the Caribbean and Panama, and investigations were ongoing. Interpol is deeply involved in some of these investigations at this time.

Notwithstanding this, I will have my operatives in the Caribbean look into this particular matter as there has been a move in recent times to get banks in Switzerland and the Caribbean to be more cooperative under certain circumstances, particularly if they were informed of a serious crime involving the account holder."

Pierre Dubois promised get back to Chief Inspector Segueras as soon as possible.

Around 5.30, *'Ivan Gudonov'* received a text message that most of the embassy staff had left for the day and the ambassador's private secretary would arrange for their security guards to let them enter in the next half hour.

Manny Rose's driver was waiting outside the hotel and when *'Ivan Gudonov'* drove out from the Hyatt Hotel car park in his rented Hyundai I-30, they followed him in the van to the nearby Russian embassy. They parked in the quiet street outside the sprawling grounds of the embassy and both men walked up to the two guards standing by the main gate. *'Ivan Gudonov'* spoke to them in Russian and after checking with the appropriate Embassy official they let them both enter. At the door to the office complex, they were both subjected to screening with a metal detector, then searched for any non-metallic objects that could cause bodily harm. Once inside, a smartly uniformed woman greeted them and led them down a long corridor to a room with a large table and big leather chairs.

Shortly after, a man entered and was introduced as the first attaché to the ambassador who spoke excellent English… albeit with a heavy accent. He told them that the package they had stored for *'Ivan Gudonov'* would be brought in to them shortly. In the meantime, refreshments would be provided for their enjoyment, compliments of the Russian government. The woman who had greeted them at the door earlier came in with a tray that had a bottle of vodka, some glasses, a bowl of nuts and pretzels. She poured drinks for them both and left the room.

The two men sipped their drinks saying little for about 10 minutes, and then the assistant came in with two other men carrying a long package which they laid gently on the floor. They nodded to Manny Rose, spoke some words in Russian to *'Ivan Gudonov'* and left the room closing the door after them.

Alexei Nagormy then stood up, pushed some chairs out of the way and cleared an area on the floor large enough to unroll the painting for viewing.

As the painting was unfurled, Manny Rose immediately recognised the unmistakable style of Jackson Pollock, vivid splashes of colour over a vast area of canvas. It was an amazing piece of art that gave the viewer plenty to think about whilst trying to interpret what the artist was saying. He noticed that despite its round-the-world travels, the painting appeared to be undamaged thanks to the simple protection of the plastic pipe and the fabric that covering the painted surface when rolled up.

After studying the painting for about 15 minutes, Manny Rose told *'Ivan Gudonov'*, "I am extremely impressed with what you have for sale and it is my intention to recommend to my father that we proceed with the purchase. Under the circumstances as detailed by you in respect to the outstanding provenance, we would require you to sign a document agreeing to refund the money on return of the painting should the provenance not be provided within 30 days from the date the final payment of US$9 million has been paid."

He went on, "We will have the document prepared overnight by our legal department and if you call me at 10 am tomorrow, we can arrange to meet and make the final payment." Alexei Nagormy smiled and told Manny Rose it was a pleasure doing business with him.

This was the first and possibly the last time Alexei Nagormy would be seen smiling. It was assumed that he was being provided with accommodation at the Embassy because the AFP had contacted all Canberra hotels and he had not checked in at any of them under either name.

The painting was carefully rolled up again and Alexei Nagormy pushed a button on the wall to summons the attaché to collect the painting and escort Manny from the embassy. Alexei Nagormy was ecstatic now it appeared that he had finally sold the stolen painting and intended to celebrate later with his friends at the embassy. They said goodnight and Manny was taken to the main gate and waved through by the one of the security guards who even managed to crack a smile.

He returned to his car and asked the driver to take him to the Rydges Hotel where the others were all now back there and waiting to hear what had transpired at the Russian Embassy.

He met up with Sergeant O'Donnell, Martin and Carlos in one of the private lounges in the hotel where they wouldn't be observed just in case Alexei Nagormy had had him followed. As they had only been able to observe and record the meeting at the Hyatt, Manny Rose went on to recount the events that had taken place at the Russian Embassy.

It was agreed that the remaining money be transferred to the bank account in the Cayman Islands overnight. The special document relating to return of the purchase price requiring *'Ivan Gudonov's'* signature was to be prepared by the company's lawyers first thing in the morning.

Manny Rose was to contact him as soon as the second payment had been transferred to the account in the Cayman Islands. Once the bank had confirmed receipt, arrangements were to be made for Manny Rose to meet him at the Russian Embassy to collect the painting. Once the painting was safely in the van, he was to follow Manny Rose to the Southern Cross office where the special document was waiting for his signature. This would finalize the deal between them.

Manny Rose told the gathering, "I have arranged for a full size van to take me to the embassy so we can lay the rolled up painting on the floor in the back. I have requested my people to have a large foam mattress placed on the floor to cushion any bumps during the painting's journey from the embassy."

Sergeant O'Donnell then advised the group, "The AFP would provide unmarked cars to accompany the van from the Russian Embassy to the Southern Cross office which I have just been informed is located in the commercial centre of Canberra. They are not to lose sight of Alexei Nagormy in his rented car or the van and its precious cargo until it is safely inside the underground garage at Manny Rose's office." My men will arrest Alexei Nagormy as he is about to leave the Southern Cross office and charge him with entering Australia on a false passport and being in possession of an alleged stolen item of art."

They had dinner sent up to the private lounge and around 10 o'clock Manny Rose departed for the hotel where he was staying, and the others went up to their rooms.

....

CHAPTER 19

CANBERRA OCTOBER 29

Martin and Carlos were up early to discuss the forthcoming culmination of their efforts to catch Alexei and repossess the stolen painting. This was going to be a momentous day and they both needed to report the positive news from the latest events to their respective chiefs.

After breakfast, they were joined by the AFP representative Sergeant O'Donnell and he explained in detail the arrangements that had been put in place to ensure that Alexei Nagormy did not slip away as he had in the other countries when he had managed to stay a step ahead of the local police. "As I have mentioned previously, this operation has the full backing of the Australian government and is being treated as a major crime requiring our best resources. We have AFP personnel stationed in the streets around the Russian embassy posing as some of the many tourists who wander around photographing the embassy buildings. These embassies in Canberra are a wonderful collection of styles. We also have the Southern Cross office building completely surrounded by AFP personnel in unmarked police cars and a number of people are also inside the building posing as staff. There is an underground car-park and the entrance is now manned with AFP security people."

He continued, "We do not anticipate that he will be carrying any firearms and because the arrest will take place in the Southern Cross private underground garage, there is no chance of any danger to the public. The building already has an impressive array of high quality CCTV cameras installed, and every movement into and out of the building is continuously monitored."

Promptly at 10am, Manny Rose received a call from Alexei Nagormy to say that he had logged on to his account at the Cayman Island bank and confirmed the balance of the money had been deposited.

"I will have the painting packed back in the plastic pipe and ready for collection from the Russian embassy promptly at 10 minutes before midday. It is important that you are not late as the embassy closes at midday and does not reopen until 2.00pm." Manny Rose replied, "I will be coming in a rented Ford Transit van with my chauffeur and the registration number is LFA-474. Please make arrangements for us to be able to drive into the front car-park at the Russian Embassy to collect the painting." He went on, "Our lawyer has prepared the document you need to sign and it is at our company office in town. You can follow our van there when we leave the Embassy. Alexei Nagormy immediately objected and asked, "Why couldn't the document be brought to the Embassy for me to sign there?"

Manny Rose replied, "The reason I asked you to come to our office is because I wanted our lawyer to be on hand to make any changes if you were not satisfied with the wording." Despite not being happy with this arrangement, he reluctantly agreed that this made sense and in any case, he was desperate to finalize the sale and return to Moscow as soon as possible. He abruptly replied, "I will only meet with you and the lawyer, no other people are to be present."

Manny Rose told him that was acceptable. "We will be at the embassy at 10 minutes before midday to take delivery of the painting, so we'll see you then. If the Embassy guard needs to record the name of the chauffeur, it is Tony Roberts and he is an employee of Southern Cross."

He then called Sergeant O'Donnell using an office phone rather than his mobile in case the Russians were somehow monitoring his calls, and told him of the time he was to go to the Embassy. He then installed the company lawyer in the board room and reviewed the document of sale with the special clause relating to the return of the ten million dollars if no genuine provenance was provided within 30 days. Satisfied with the wording, he thanked the lawyer and then went down to the car-park to look at the van the chauffeur had picked up earlier that morning.

It was brand new and the only external marking was the Hertz sign on the rear window.

A thick foam mattress had been laid on the floor and there were no loose objects floating around that could roll into the plastic pipe containing the painting as they travelled from the embassy to the office.

Returning to the office, he called his father to update him on the latest events and before hanging up, told him, "What a pity it is that the painting is stolen property because it would really look fantastic hanging in our head office boardroom!"

Just after 11.30, Manny called the chauffeur to meet him in the car-park and drive him to the Russian Embassy.

At precisely 10 minutes to 12, the white Ford Transit pulled up to the gates at the Russian Embassy. The guard checked the van number and the identity of the two occupants. They had to get out of the van whilst the guard ran his wand over them to check for weapons then made a thorough search of the empty van.

Once he was satisfied that these two men were *'clean'* he waved them through to the tradesman's entrance located around the side of the main building.

The guard must have called Alexei Nagormy to let him know that the visitors had arrived because he was standing outside the building in front of an open roller door as they drove around the corner. This section of the building appeared to be a warehouse of some kind.

After a few curt words had been exchanged concerning Canberra's cool weather, two men appeared carrying the long plastic pipe. The rear door of the van was raised and they laid the pipe carefully on the carpet. Manny removed the end cap from the pipe and gently eased the contents forward so he could check that this was actually the Jackson Pollock painting.

He didn't expect that there would be any trickery at this stage but having outlaid 10 million dollars of the company's money, he wanted to be certain that everything was *'kosher'*. Once he was satisfied that all was as it should be, he closed and locked the van's rear door and told Alexei Nagormy, "Mr. Gudonov, please follow me to the Southern Cross office in the city to sign the special document of sale. Our business will then be finalized."

The van with Alexei Nagormy's rental car following close behind departed the embassy together and headed for downtown. Unbeknownst to the Russian, the progress of the two vehicles along Canberra's wide avenues was being monitored by AFP officers sitting in a chartered traffic report helicopter high above them. As well, there were unmarked cars in front and behind. This was done for two reasons... firstly to ensure nothing untoward happened to this extremely valuable painting and secondly to maintain surveillance of Alexei Nagormy who had proven over and over again just how slippery he can be.

Some 15 minutes later, the vehicles turned into the underground garage at the Southern Cross Shopping Centres office and parked side by side near the lift where two spaces had been intentionally marked *'Reserved for Special Guests'*. When the elevator arrived and the doors opened, Alexei

Nagormy nervously looked all around to see if anyone else was there and was noticeably relieved when he saw it was empty.

He found himself uncomfortable with these arrangements as he was accustomed to being in full control of his surroundings and this situation was not to his liking. Although he couldn't see anyone suspicious standing around or anything obviously out of place, things did not feel right to him. He was beginning to regret that he had agreed to come here but there was nothing he could do now but have the formalities completed as quickly as possible and get the hell out of Canberra as fast as he could. The chauffeur and Manny Rose carefully lifted the heavy pipe containing the painting into the elevator and because of its length had to stand it upright at an angle so the doors could close. Manny Rose, Alexei Nagormy and the chauffeur rode to the top floor where the boardroom was located.

Once the painting was laid on the floor along a wall, the chauffeur was excused and Manny buzzed the company lawyer to come to the boardroom.

After introducing Alexei Nagormy to the lawyer, the special document was tabled and he was requested to read it and if satisfied with the wording, he was then to sign above his printed name. Naturally, it was written in legal jargon which he found difficult to fully understand but after the lawyer slowly explained the meaning of each sentence, Alexei Nagormy agreed to sign it with the name he was using in Australia....Ivan Gudonov. This of course meant that the document would not stand up in court and Alexei Nagormy smiled inwardly believing he had got the better of this smart-arse family! Manny Rose knew this was all show and that Alexei Nagormy had no intention of ever honouring the agreement but remained straight faced in order not to let on.

The lawyer took the document to make a copy for Alexei Nagormy and whilst he was out of the room, Manny Rose took a bottle of vodka out from the director's bar and poured a couple of shots to close the deal.

Alexei downed his drink in one quick gulp and then asked if he could be excused as soon as possible because he had booked a flight to Hong Kong leaving Sydney that evening and had a number of things to finalize before then.

The lawyer returned with the copy of the document for the Russian and then Manny Rose escorted him down to the basement garage. As the elevator doors opened, Alexei Nagormy was confronted by Sergeant O'Donnell and four officers pointing guns at him. He was told that he was under arrest for smuggling a stolen painting into Australia as well as entering the country on a false passport.

He was patted down but no weapons were found and he was immediately handcuffed and placed in the back of an AFP van with no windows. He protested loudly that he had been set up and wanted to speak to the Russian Ambassador immediately. He was told that would be arranged once he was placed in custody at the AFP Canberra headquarters.

Within minutes all AFP personnel and vehicles had departed and things returned to normal at the Southern Cross offices.

The arrest was witnessed by Martin and Carlos who were standing in the shadows on the other side of the underground car-park.

It was such a well organised arrest and because there was no fighting or shooting or need to use a Taser, it seemed to be an anti-climax after he had been chased halfway around the world by the two police officers. The AFP team didn't want anyone to be hurt in any way but they had expected Alexei Nagormy to put up much more of a fight. No doubt he was also exhausted after all the travelling he had done and the many time zones crossed. In any case, he was sure that his connections would quickly arrange to have him released and returned to Russia. Besides, the ten million dollars was now safely in his secret bank account.

The car rental firm that had provided Alexei Nagormy with the I-30 was contacted and requested to come to the Southern Cross offices and collect the car as the person who had rented it was no longer in a position to return it to the airport himself.

Martin and Carlos rode the elevator to the top floor with Manny Rose and sat down with him to review how well the operation went. He was thanked at great length for the role he had played. Carlos then said, "I am pleased to pass on a message just received from the Chief Inspector in Spain. The 10 million dollars you have paid out will immediately be refunded by the insurance company and they have already instigated steps to recover the money from the Cayman Islands bank.

The insurance company will also reimburse Southern Cross Shopping Centres for any other costs incurred over the past two days. I will give you the Bilbao Police Headquarters email address for you to advise your banking details in order for them to have the funds transferred promptly."

Despite it being the early hours of the morning in Europe, Carlos called Bilbao and spoke to the Chief Inspector to tell him the good news.

In a somewhat sleepy voice, Señor Segueras told Carlos, "We believe that the Spanish government will immediately commence extradition proceedings with the Australian government and this could take some time. Because of Alexei Nagormy's connections with the Russian hierarchy, there will no doubt be a legal battle that could drag on for months. You may be required to return to Australia at a later date to accompany him to Bilbao once the Australian government has agreed to the extradition request. In the meantime, you are to prepare to return to Spain as soon as arrangements can be made. Our Ambassador in Canberra has been instructed to assist you in any way you need. All of Spain is abuzz with your exploits in tracking down and finally capturing this criminal. Martin Taylor is also being lauded by the press in Europe. We look forward to seeing you back home soon." Carlos replied, "A lot of credit must be given to the role played by the Australian Federal Police for the manner they handled the operation starting with their involvement in Sydney and concluding with the arrest here in Canberra. I was impressed by their professionalism from start to finish."

Martin called the Melbourne police headquarters and told the Police Commissioner about the arrest and asked for a flight to be booked for him to return to Melbourne the next day.

That evening, a celebration dinner was held at Canberra's swankiest restaurant arranged and paid for by the Spanish Ambassador, Señor Enrico del Francisco. Martin, Carlos, Sergeant O'Donnell and Manny Rose rode in a stretch limousine to the restaurant where over a delicious meal, our two *'heroes'* recounted the adventures that had started for them less than three weeks ago but now seemed like months.

Sergeant O'Donnell told them that the news of the arrest had been broadcast on the evening news and would be on the front page of all Australian newspapers tomorrow morning. "We will deliver the Jackson Pollock painting to the Spanish Embassy tomorrow for safe-keeping until it can be returned to Spain and included in the exhibition at the Guggenheim Museum in Bilbao."

He continued after a sip of the Spanish wine ordered by the Ambassador, "We will be providing copies of all the surveillance CCTV videos and audio tapes from the meeting between Manny Rose and Alexei Nagormy at the Hyatt Hotel which could be used in the trial against him whenever that takes place. At this stage, very few details have been given to the press other than advising them that a valuable painting stolen a few weeks ago in Spain had been recovered in Canberra and that a Russian national had been arrested in connection with the theft and his subsequent attempt to sell it here."

He went on, "At the request of the Australian Foreign Minister, no mention has been made of any involvement by the Russian Embassy. Notwithstanding, the Russian ambassador has telephoned the Foreign Affairs Department claiming that the embassy had been unaware that the painting they had been asked to store for a few days had been stolen. It had been brought into Australia as a diplomatic package under a request from a government official in Moscow and assigned to a Mr. Alexei Nagormy. The embassy was also unaware that he had entered Australia under the name of Ivan Gudonov using a false passport. The ambassador apologised for the embassy having been involved in this alleged crime and promised to assist in any way they could to bring the matter to a close."

The ambassador had then requested that embassy staff be given access to speak with Alexei wherever he was being held so that they could arrange for him to have legal representation. It seems that Alexei was being held at a special AFP holding cell in the Canberra suburb of Belconnen. This gaol was used for detaining criminals arrested in Canberra on charges for crimes carried out in any of the Australian states or territories until it had been decided in which state the trial would take place. It also housed foreigners who have been caught entering the country illegally or were wanted overseas on serious charges before they were deported back to their country of residence.

A short time later, Carlos stood up to make another speech, "Everyone here as well as my colleagues in Spain wish to thank Manny Rose for his very important role in the capture of the Russian and we wish him to convey to his family our appreciation of the assistance given by them."

Martin then asked, "Has the AFP learned anything more about Alexei's background. We know he has an import export business in antiques and old rugs but why did he suddenly appear to venture into stolen art?"

Sergeant O'Donnell replied, "We have discussed this with our people working at the Australian Embassy in Moscow and it seems that Alexei gained a reputation some years back of being able to get his hands on all kinds of valuable art objects usually on request from customers he has done business with previously. Because of his connections at the highest levels of government he has been able to avoid being charged and convicted of any crimes. We can only hope that this time justice will prevail!"

The party broke up around midnight and everyone bade each other farewell hoping to meet again one day. Martin and Carlos told the gathering that they would certainly meet again as Martin would be required to attend the murder trial in Bilbao. Now that the mastermind behind the theft of the painting and the associated murder had been caught, it was expected that the trial would commence a few months after Alexei Nagormy has been extradited to Spain.

Back at the Rydges hotel, Martin arranged to have breakfast with Carlos and then they would travel to the airport together. The Spanish embassy had booked flights for Carlos to return to Spain. He was to fly with Qantas to Sydney then catch an Emirates flight to Madrid via Dubai. Martin was flying back to Melbourne.

They had become very close friends during the past few weeks and although they were delighted to have closed off the case successfully, they were a little sad to be parting company. Of course Carlos was missing his family and was really looking forward to seeing them again. He intended to take some time off on his return to make up for being away from them for so long.

Martin on the other hand was actually looking forward to returning to his Melbourne office and getting involved in the assignments we had been told were piling up on his desk.

....

CHAPTER 20

MELBOURNE OCTOBER 30

Martin flew into Melbourne around mid-morning the next day and took a cab straight to the new police complex in the World Trade Centre located in the Docklands precinct. They had moved here from the old building in St.Kilda Road whilst Martin was overseas so this was his first look at the new facilities. It would be nice working in new surroundings he decided but unfortunately the location was not as convenient to the art galleries, concert hall and theatres. His assistant told him that the State Government had signed an agreement with a developer to build an entirely new facility in nearby Spencer Street that would be 'state of the art' and would house all branches of the Victorian Police in the one multi-storey building. It would be designed to include the best available security equipment and anti-terrorist bomb and bullet proof materials in its construction. This would take at least two years to build so they would be staying at the Docklands headquarters for a while yet. After a few minutes being greeted by some colleagues, he went straight up to meet with Sir Charles MacPherson, the Chief Commissioner of Police.

He was congratulated on his dedication in helping to solve this crime, and although the initial crime occurred in another country, the capture of the master-mind had taken place in Australia and had received world-wide attention.

Sir Charles told Martin, "I had another call from Chief Inspector Segueras of the Bilbao police department thanking me for allowing you to remain on the case until its satisfactory conclusion. The Spanish Government intended to award you with a certificate of gratitude that would be signed by His Highness, King Juan Carlos and the Prime Minister."

He continued, "You are to spend the rest of the week completing a detailed report on the symposium that was the real reason you were sent to Spain. Once you have finished that, you are then to prepare a separate report covering the stolen painting and the murder you witnessed on the Bilbao Funicular. This report is to start from witnessing the murder and your subsequent involvement working with the Bilbao police in tracking down and capturing the mastermind behind the crime."

Martin also needed to fill in a somewhat large expense account and had to hunt through his luggage looking for the mountain of receipts he had collected as he travelled around the world pursuing Alexei Nagormy. The Spanish insurance company had advised the Victorian police that they would also reimburse them for these costs.

The expense account was made all the more difficult to fill out because all of the countries he had visited had different currencies.

The hotels and restaurant bills that he had charged to his Visa credit card were simple as they had already been converted to Australian dollars in the card statement. It was the receipts for things he had paid cash for with local currency which had to be converted and that would take him some time to work out. Fortunately these days, the internet has made calculations like these a lot simpler and being unaccustomed to international travel, he was amazed when he eventually arrived at how much he had spent.

Tomorrow, he planned to call his team together and examine the cases that had arisen since he had departed for Spain. Once he is back into his regular work routine, possibly in the next two weeks, he is to prepare a lecture to present to the various department heads at the police headquarters complex relating to all the issues that arose during the search and hunting down of the criminals involved in the Bilbao mystery.

That night as he settled back into his apartment, he reflected on the experiences he had encountered over the past month and the lessons learned that he could now impart to his team as they went about their daily tasks.

Before going to bed, he checked his emails and was thrilled to see one from Isabella saying that she had been invited to an international law conference that was to be held in the Melbourne Convention Centre two months from now. This would give him an opportunity to show her around his home town and he was already turning over in his mind where he would take her while she was there.

It would depend on how many spare days she would have outside of the conference to fit in all the places he wanted to take her. He suddenly remembered that there was a possible complication that could arise. If the trial of Alexei Nagormy and the killer commenced in Bilbao around the same time as Isabella's planned visit to Melbourne, Martin could find himself there to give evidence instead of being in Melbourne. He hoped this scenario didn't occur and as he drifted off to sleep, his thoughts lingered on this raven haired beauty he had met in Bilbao and the forthcoming opportunity to re-kindle their brief relationship.

THE END

Notes: The stolen painting described in the story does not exist. To the author's knowledge, there has never been a Jackson Pollock painting called The Pole of Poles. If any painting by the famous artist did turn up, it was likely it would be purchased by a museum for a considerably higher price than what the one in the story was sold for.

www.ingramcontent.com/pod-product-compliance
Lightning Source LLC
LaVergne TN
LVHW091548060526
838200LV00036B/753